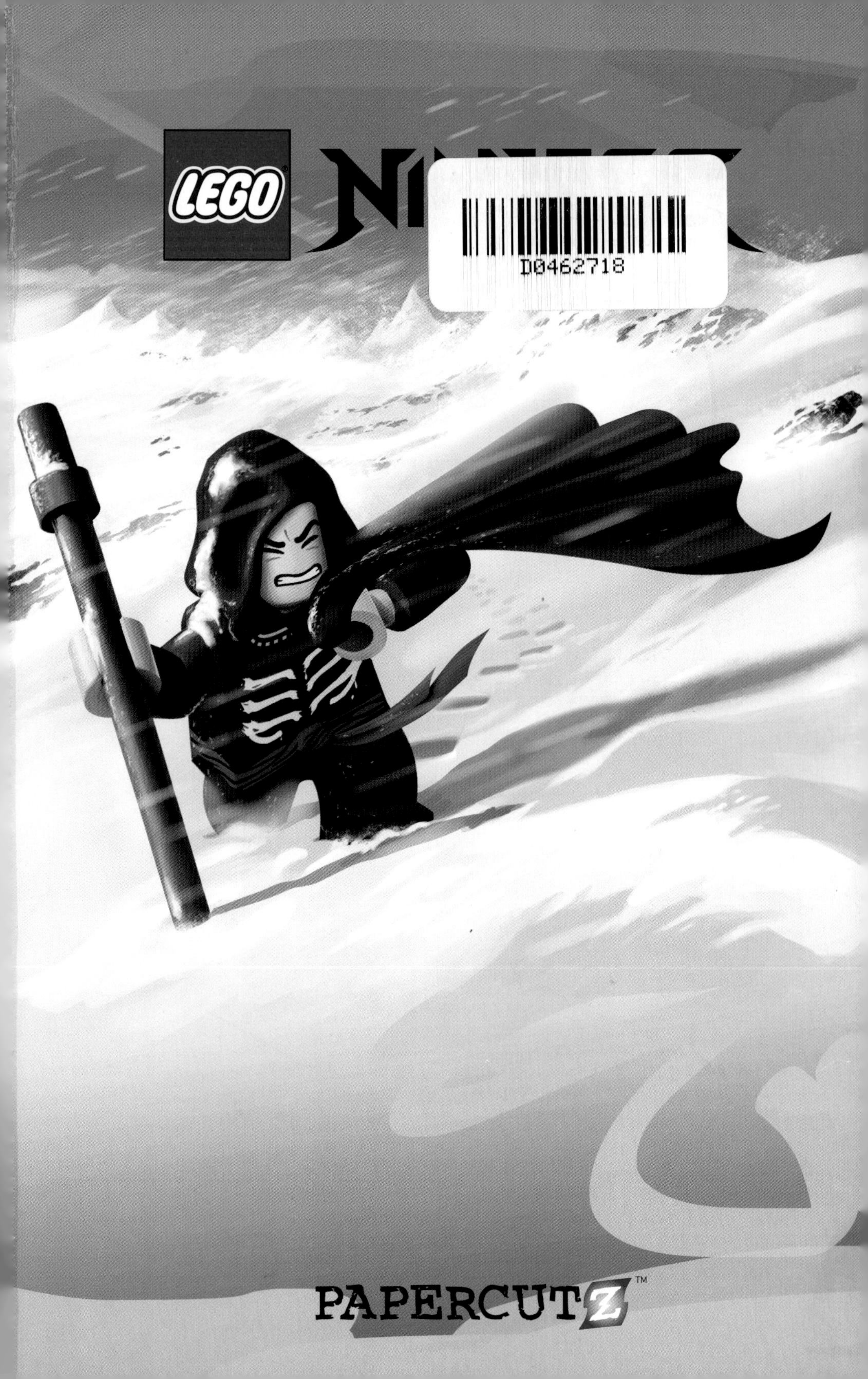
LEGO
PAPERCUTZ™

LEGO® GRAPHIC NOVELS AVAILABLE FROM PAPERCUTZ™

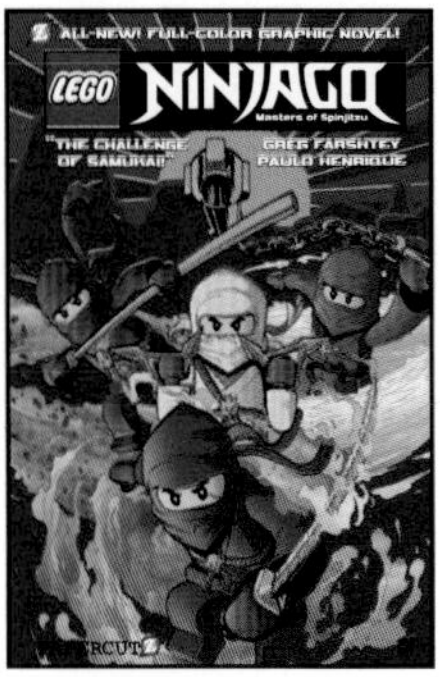
ALL-NEW! FULL-COLOR GRAPHIC NOVEL!
LEGO NINJAGO
Masters of Spinjitzu
"THE CHALLENGE OF SAMURAI"
GREG FARSHTEY
PAULO HENRIQUE
PAPERCUTZ

LEGO NINJAGO #1

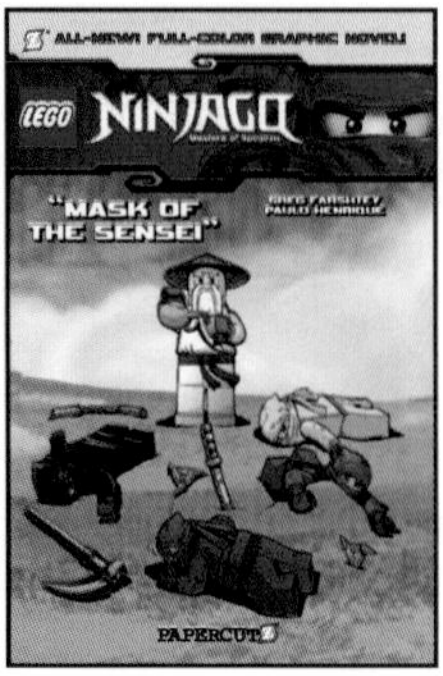
ALL-NEW! FULL-COLOR GRAPHIC NOVEL!
LEGO NINJAGO
Masters of Spinjitzu
"MASK OF THE SENSEI"
GREG FARSHTEY
PAULO HENRIQUE
PAPERCUTZ

LEGO NINJAGO #2

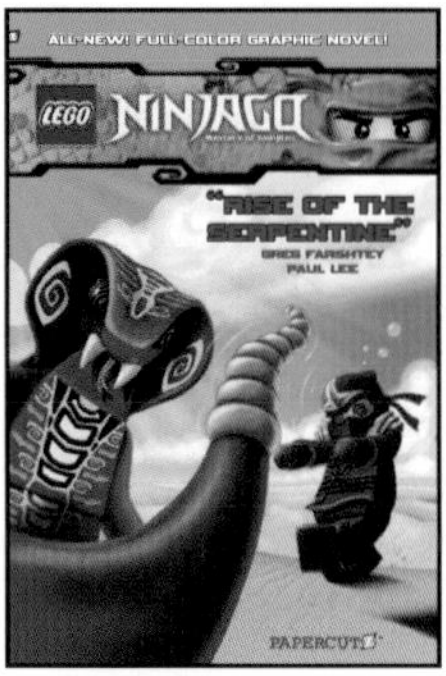
ALL-NEW! FULL-COLOR GRAPHIC NOVEL!
LEGO NINJAGO
"RISE OF THE SERPENTINE"
GREG FARSHTEY
PAUL LEE
PAPERCUTZ

LEGO NINJAGO #3

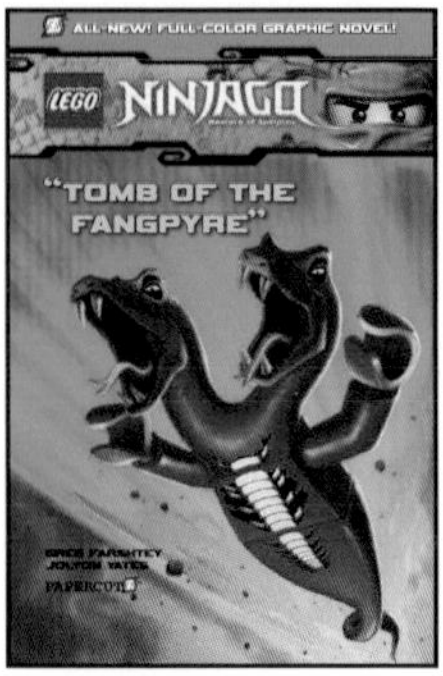
ALL-NEW! FULL-COLOR GRAPHIC NOVEL!
LEGO NINJAGO
"TOMB OF THE FANGPYRE"
GREG FARSHTEY
JOLYON YATES
PAPERCUTZ

LEGO NINJAGO #4

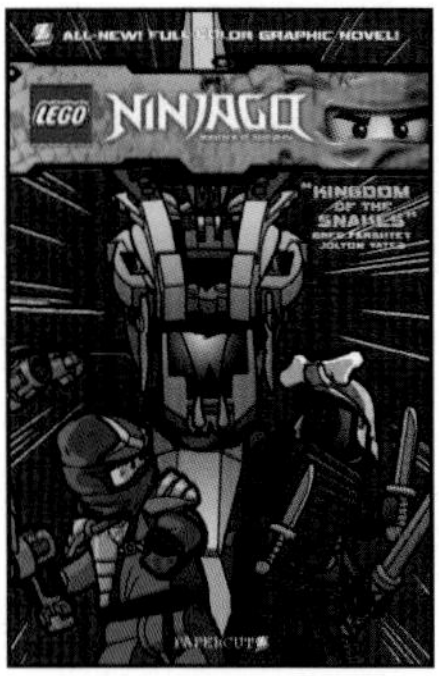
ALL-NEW! FULL-COLOR GRAPHIC NOVEL!
LEGO NINJAGO
"KINGDOM OF THE SNAKES"
GREG FARSHTEY
JOLYON YATES
PAPERCUTZ

LEGO NINJAGO #5

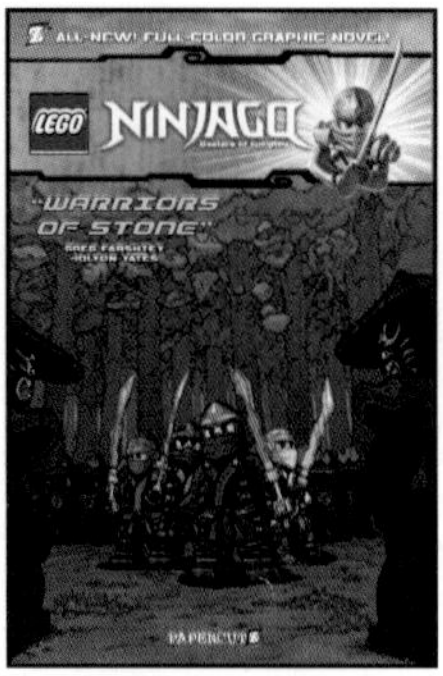
ALL-NEW! FULL-COLOR GRAPHIC NOVEL!
LEGO NINJAGO
"WARRIORS OF STONE"
GREG FARSHTEY
JOLYON YATES
PAPERCUTZ

LEGO NINJAGO #6

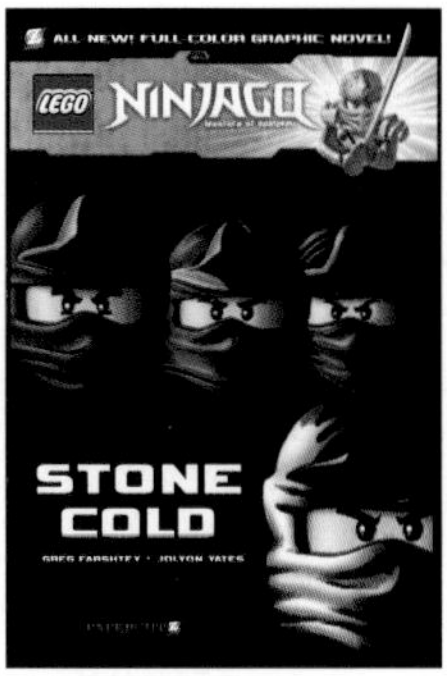
ALL-NEW! FULL-COLOR GRAPHIC NOVEL!
LEGO NINJAGO
STONE COLD
GREG FARSHTEY • JOLYON YATES
PAPERCUTZ

LEGO NINJAGO #7

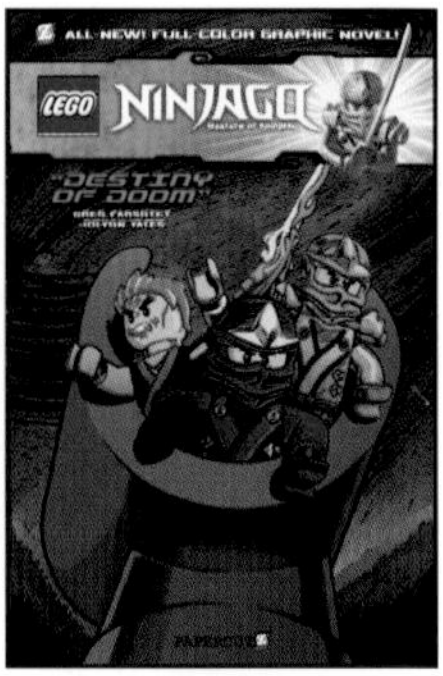
ALL-NEW! FULL-COLOR GRAPHIC NOVEL!
LEGO NINJAGO
"DESTINY OF DOOM"
GREG FARSHTEY
JOLYON YATES
PAPERCUTZ

LEGO NINJAGO #8

COMING SOON!

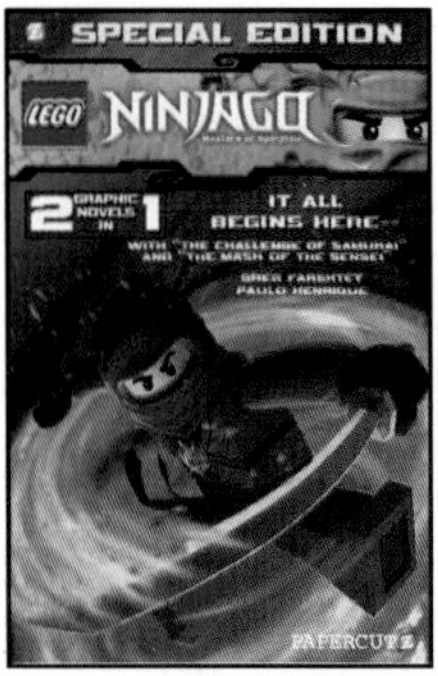
SPECIAL EDITION
LEGO NINJAGO
2 GRAPHIC NOVELS IN 1
IT ALL BEGINS HERE
PAPERCUTZ

SPECIAL EDITION #1
(Features stories from NINJAGO #1 & #2.)

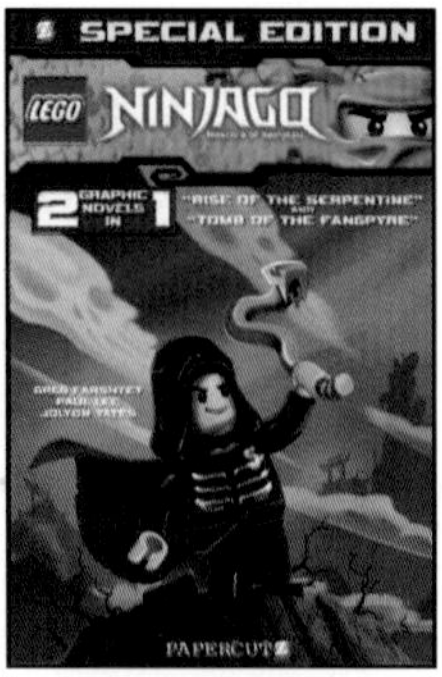
SPECIAL EDITION
LEGO NINJAGO
2 GRAPHIC NOVELS IN 1
"RISE OF THE SERPENTINE" AND "TOMB OF THE FANGPYRE"
PAPERCUTZ

SPECIAL EDITION #2
(Features stories from NINJAGO #3 & #4.)

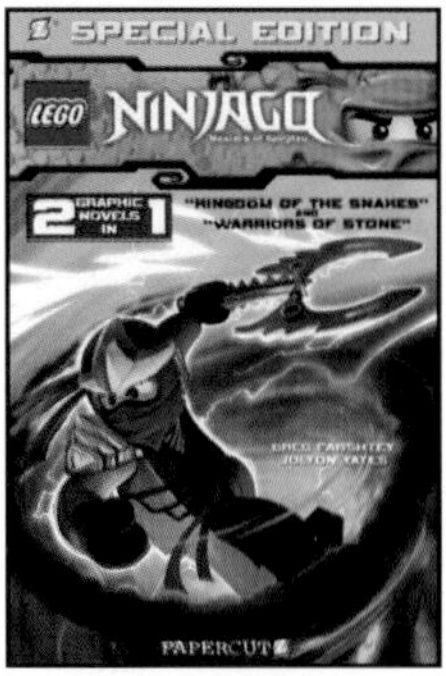
SPECIAL EDITION
LEGO NINJAGO
2 GRAPHIC NOVELS IN 1
"KINGDOM OF THE SNAKES" AND "WARRIORS OF STONE"
PAPERCUTZ

SPECIAL EDITION #3
(Features stories from NINJAGO #5 & #6.)

LEGO NINJAGO #9

LEGO® NINJAGO graphic novels are available in paperback and hardcover at booksellers everywhere.

You can also order online at papercutz.com. Or call 1-800-886-1223, Monday through Friday, 9 – 5 EST. MC, Visa, and AmEx accepted. To order by mail, please add $4.00 for postage and handling for first book ordered, $1.00 for each additional book and make check payable to NBM Publishing. Send to: Papercutz, 160 Broadway, Suite 700, East Wing, New York, NY 10038.

LEGO NINJAGO graphic novels are also available digitally wherever e-books are sold.

DESTINY OF DOOM

Greg Farshtey – Writer
Jolyon Yates – Artist
Laurie E. Smith – Colorist

New York

LEGO® NINJAGO Masters of Spinjitzu
#8 "Destiny of Doom"

GREG FARSHTEY – Writer
JOLYON YATES – Artist
LAURIE E. SMITH – Colorist
BRYAN SENKA – Letterer
DAWN K. GUZZO – Production
BETH SCORZATO – Production Coordinator
STAN LEE & JACK KIRBY – Special Thanks
MICHAEL PETRANEK – Associate Editor
JIM SALICRUP
Editor-in-Chief

ISBN: 978-1-59707-481-0 paperback edition
ISBN: 978-1-59707-480-3 hardcover edition

Papercutz books may be purchased for business or promotional use. For information on bulk purchases please contact Macmillan
Corporate and Premium Sales Department at (800) 221-7945 x5442.

Printed in the USA
August 2013 by Lifetouch Printing
5126 Forest Hills Ct.
Loves Park, IL 61111

Distributed by Macmillan

First Printing

FSC
www.fsc.org
MIX
Paper from
responsible sources
FSC® C112431

MEET THE MASTERS OF SPINJITZU...

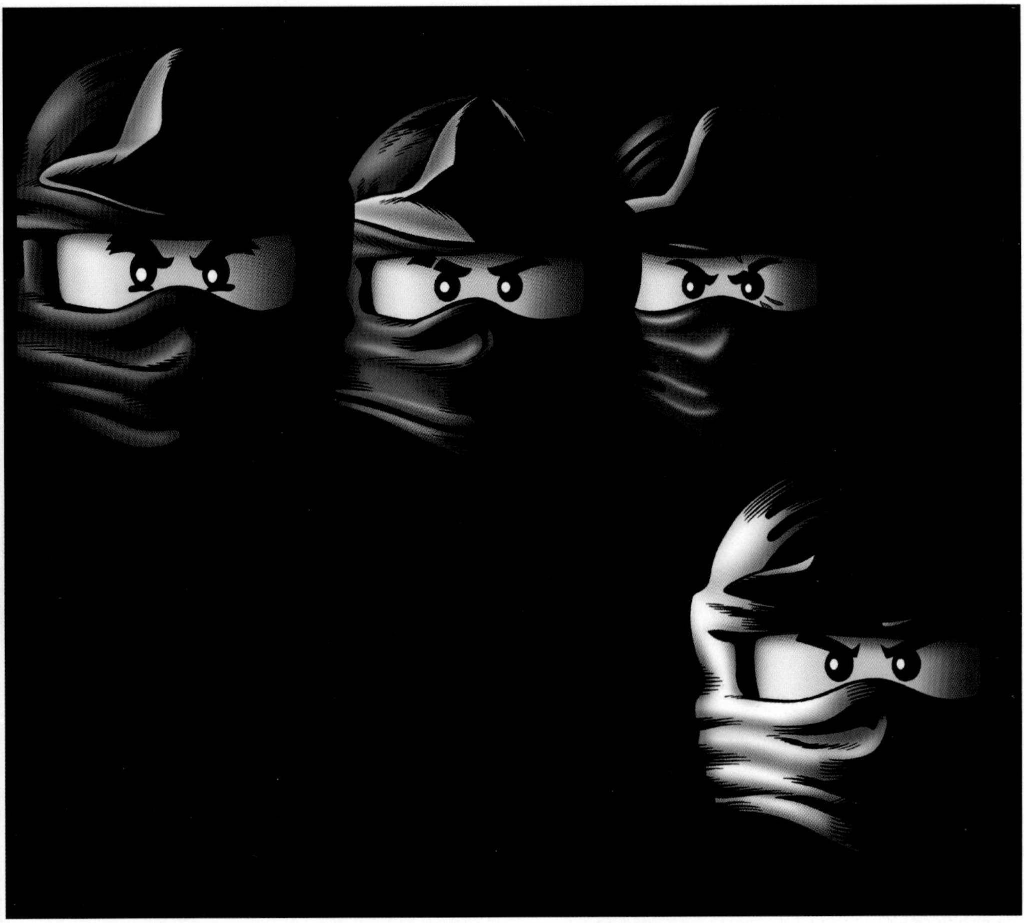

JAY

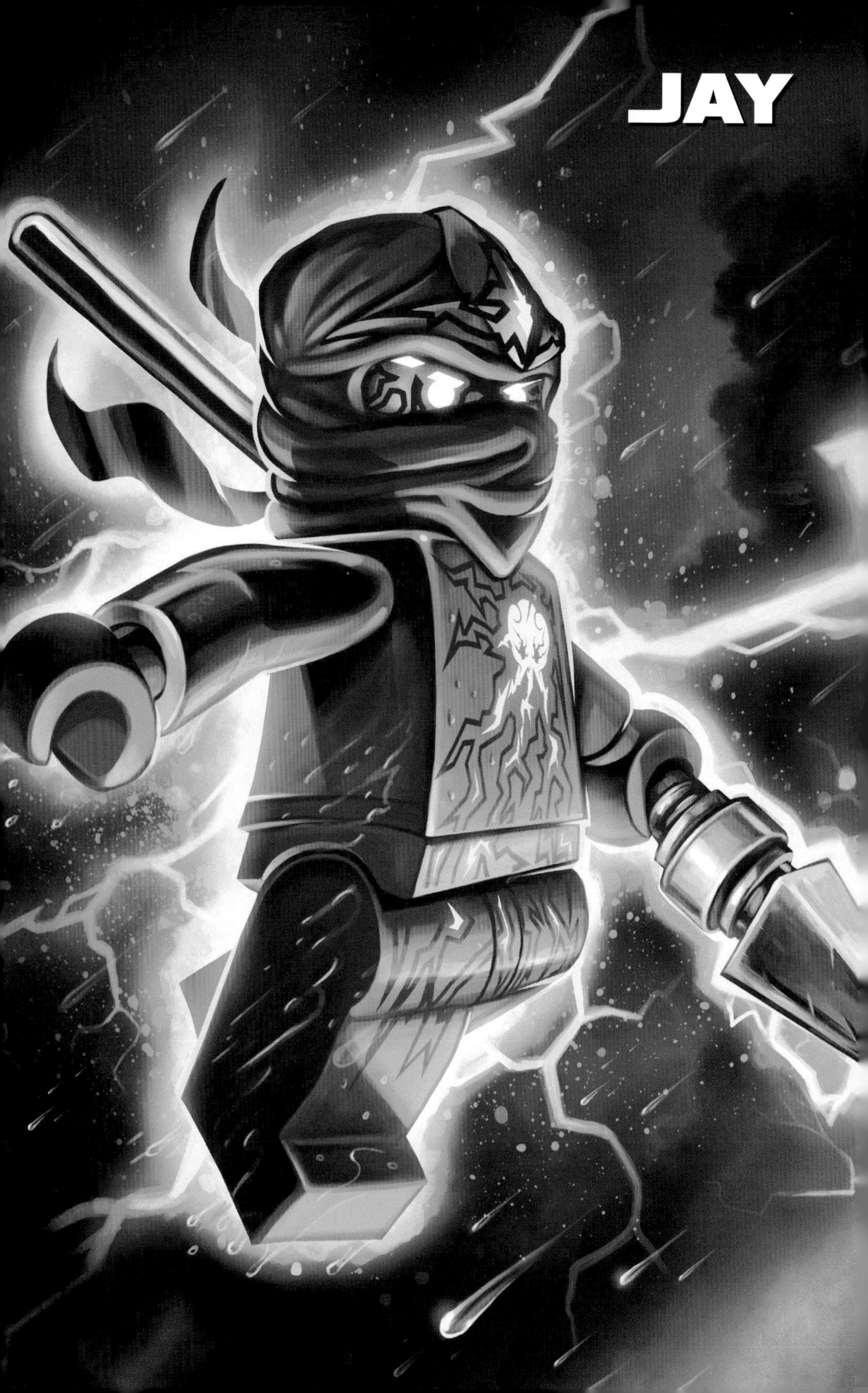

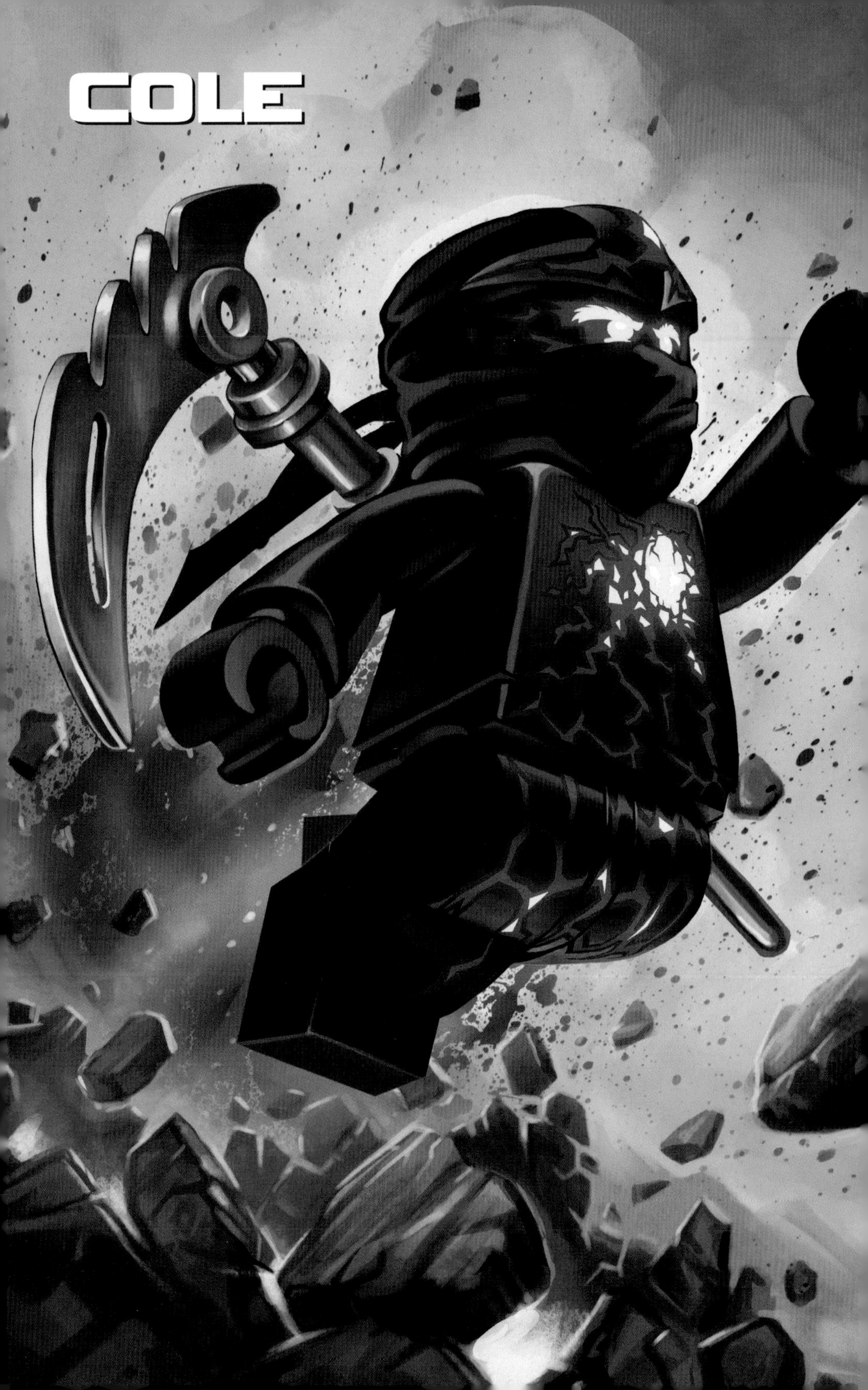
COLE

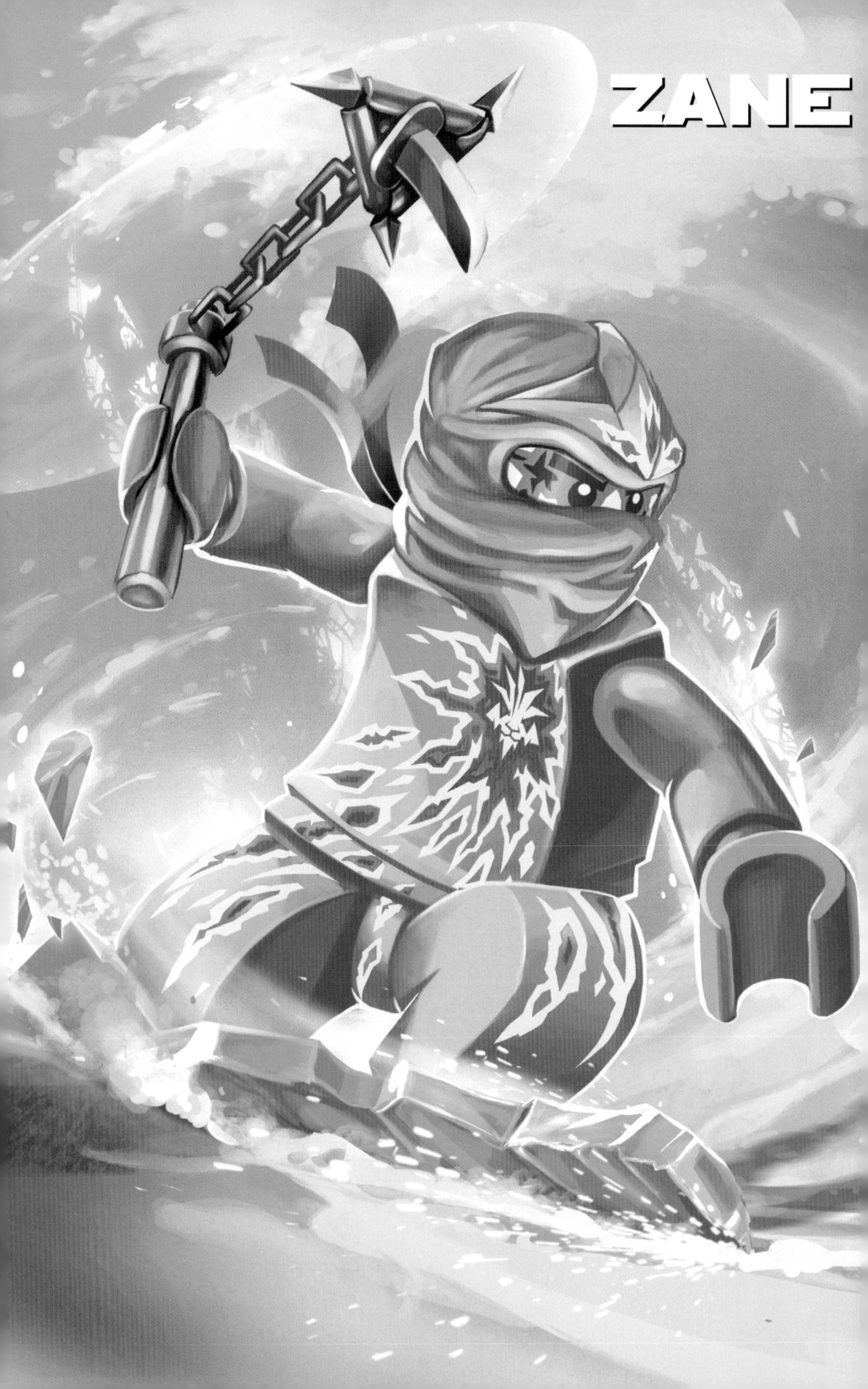
ZANE

KAI

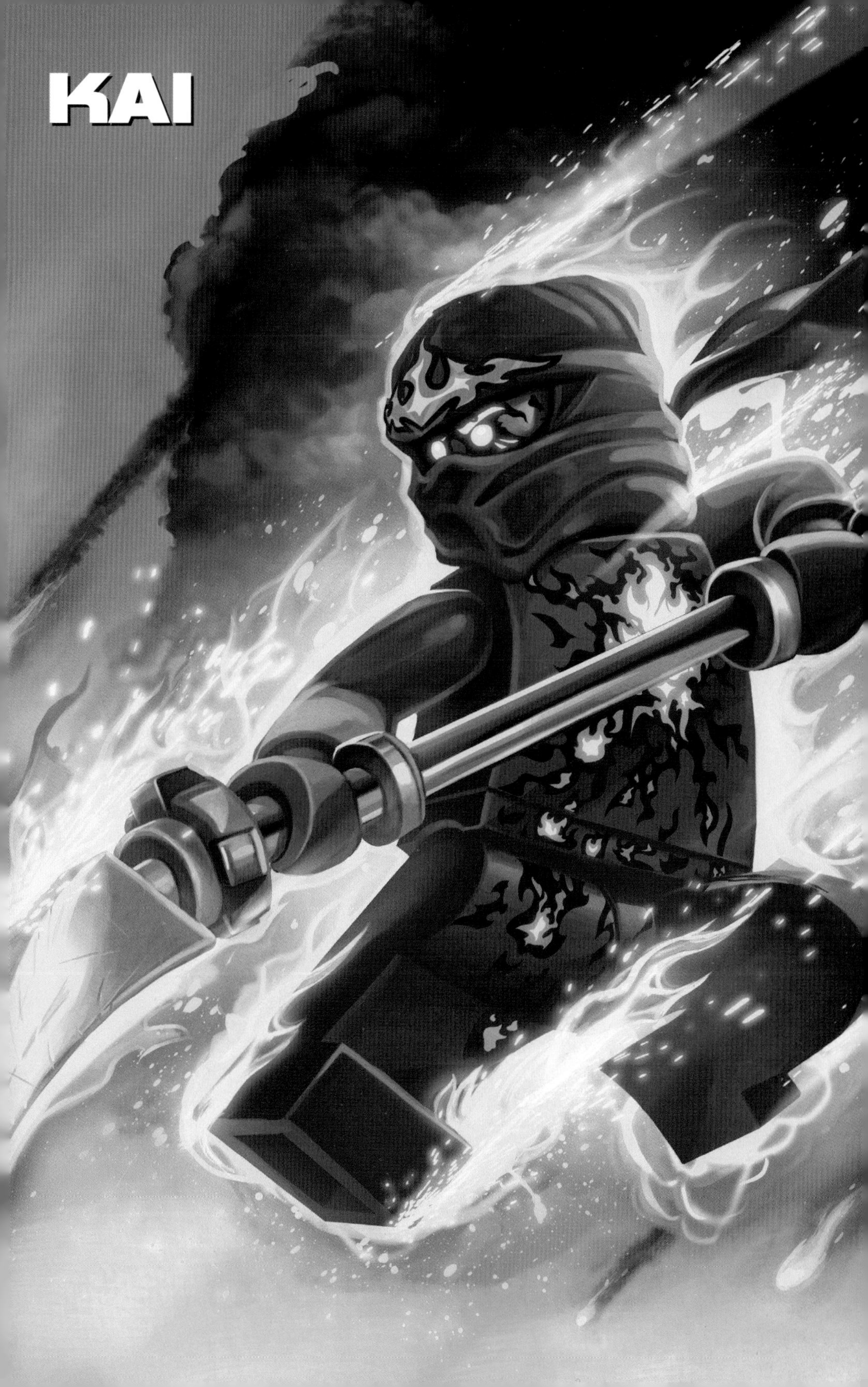

LLOYD

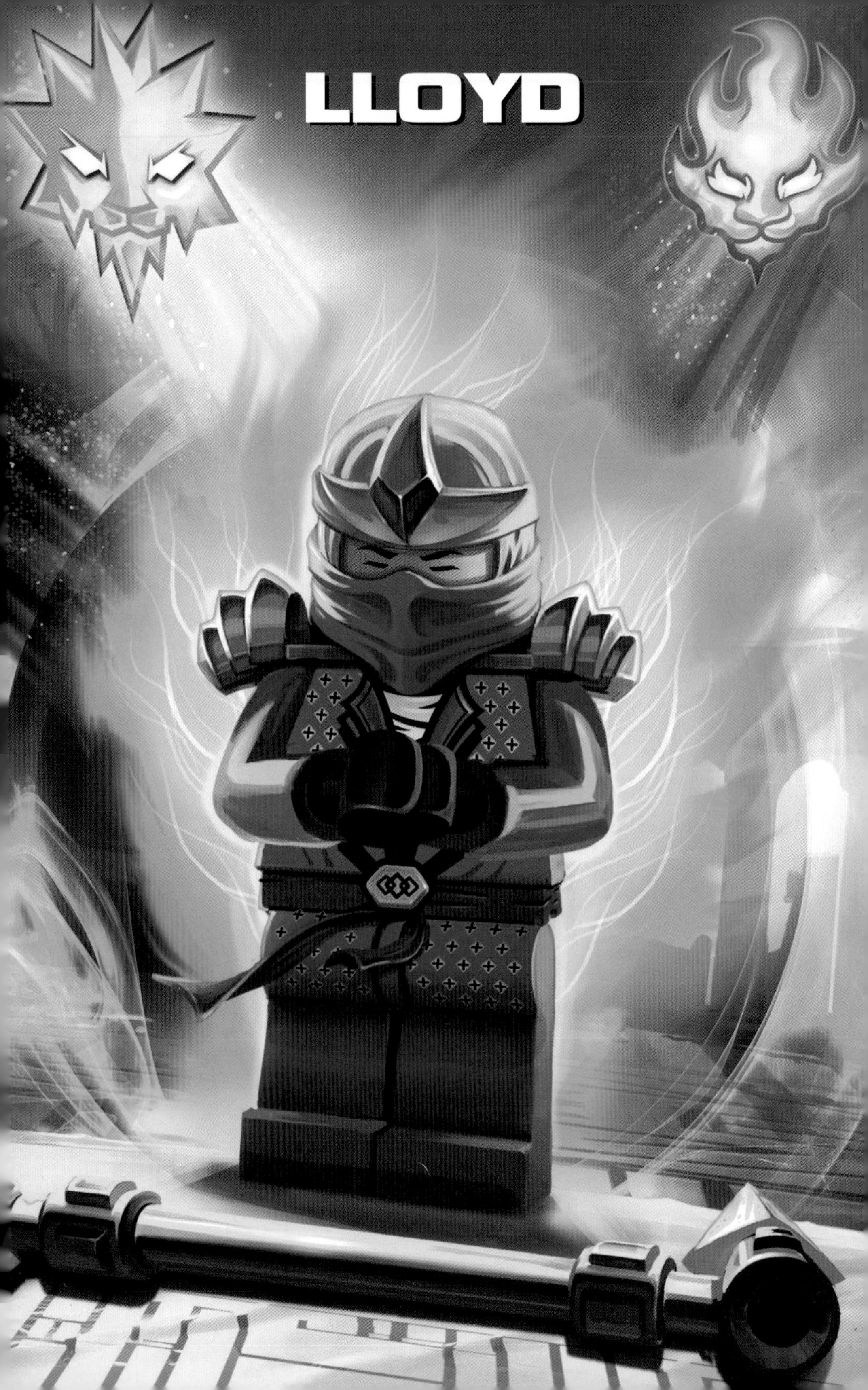

And the Master of the Masters of Spinjitzu...

SENSEI WU

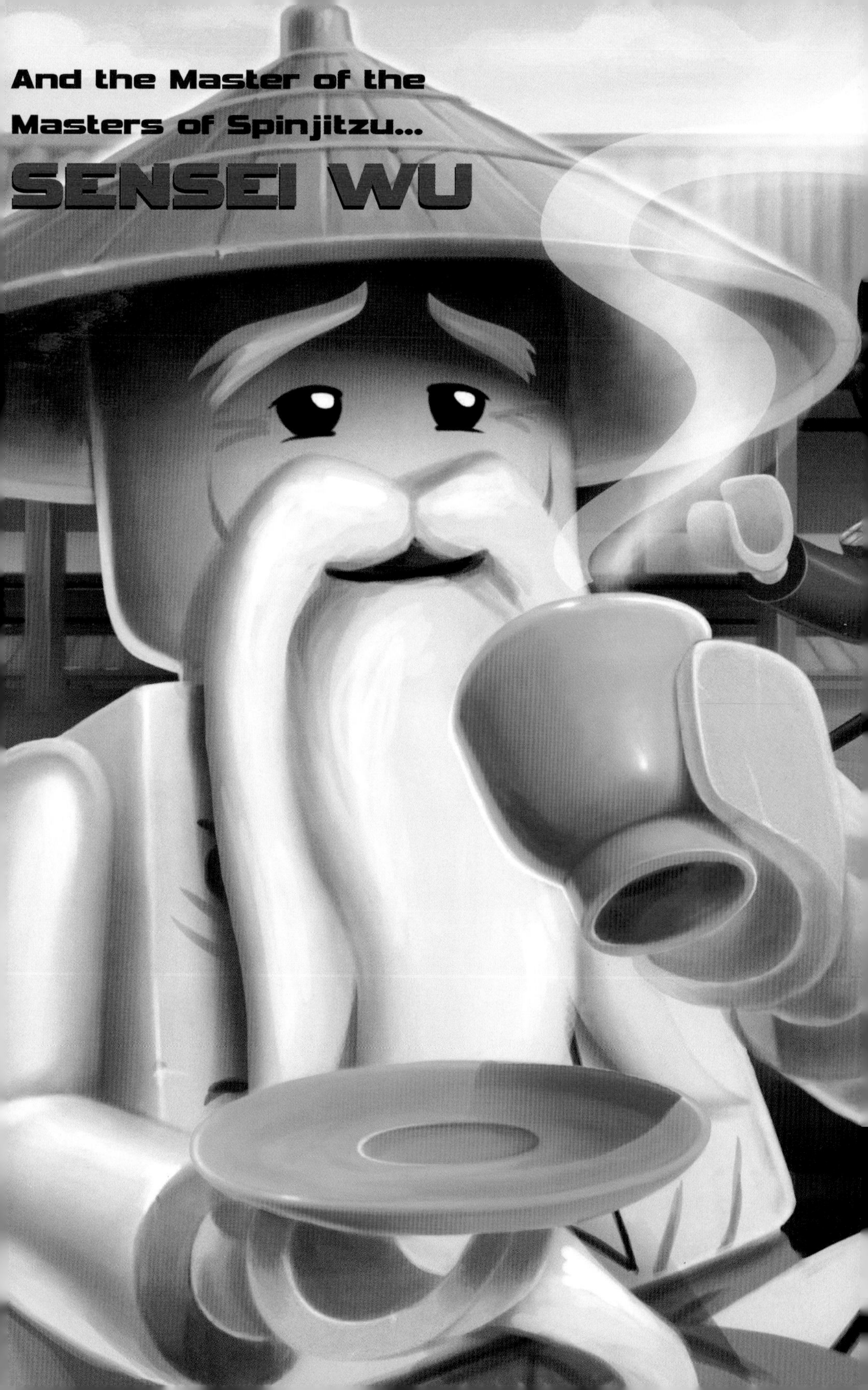

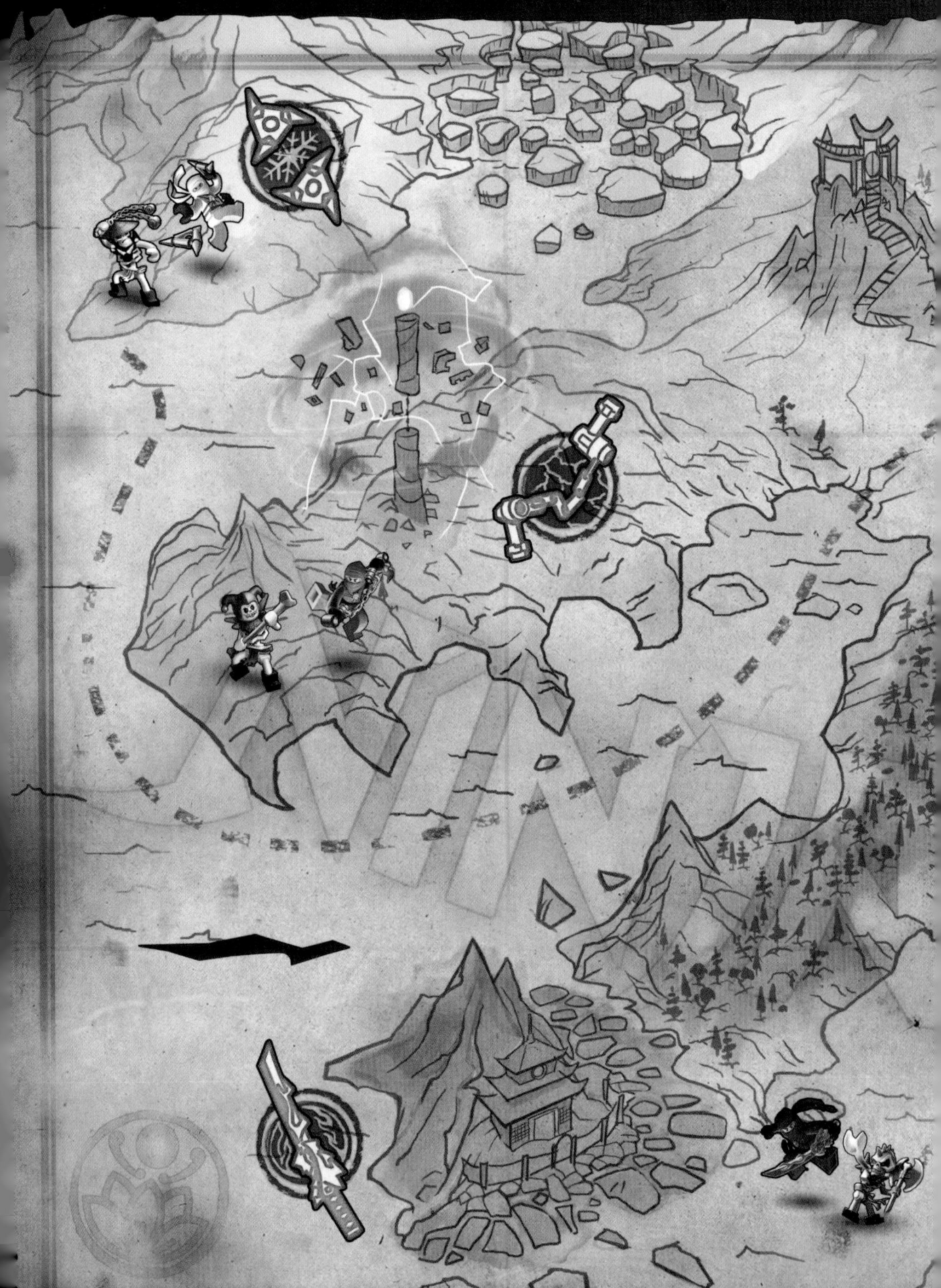

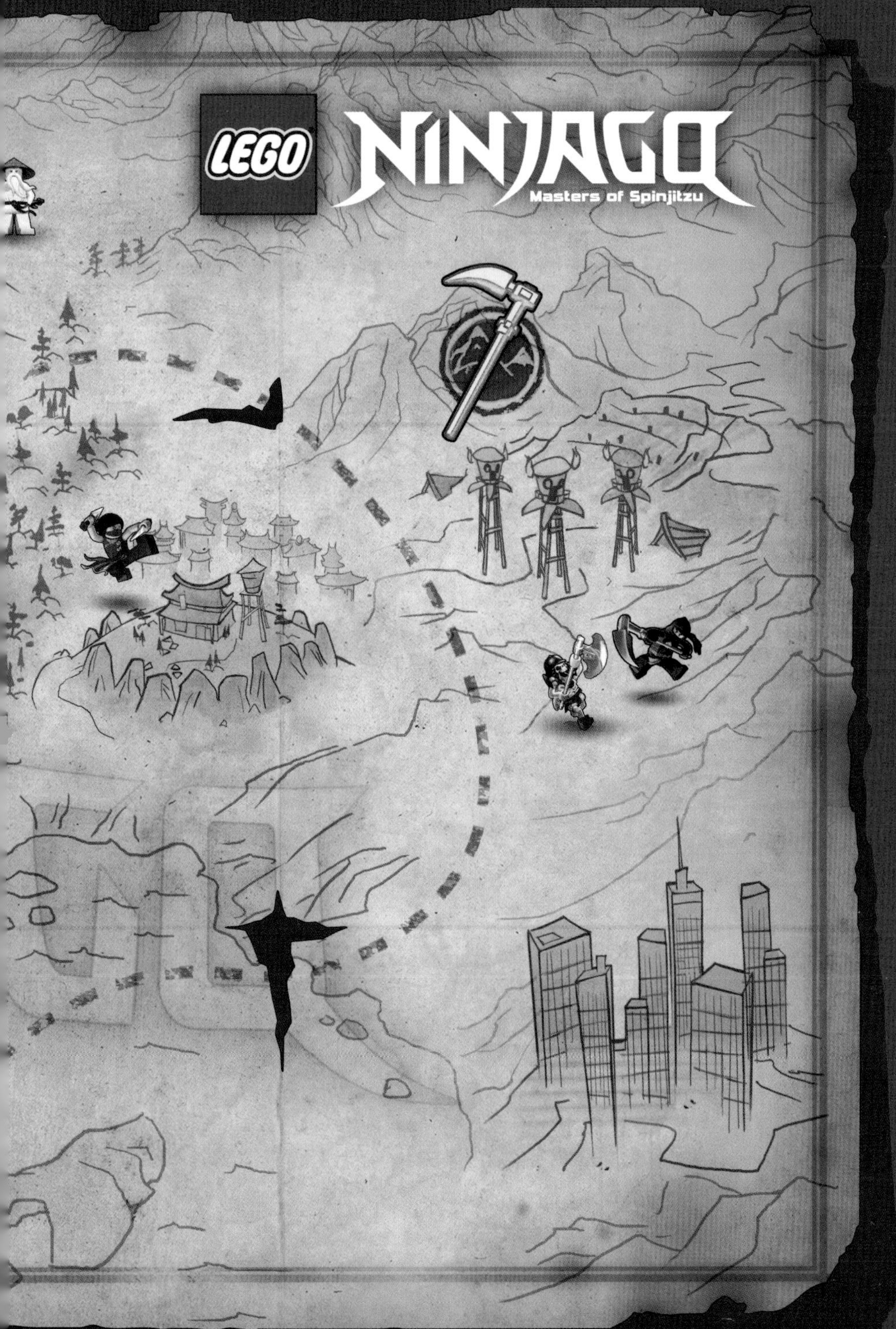
LEGO
NINJAGO
Masters of Spinjitzu

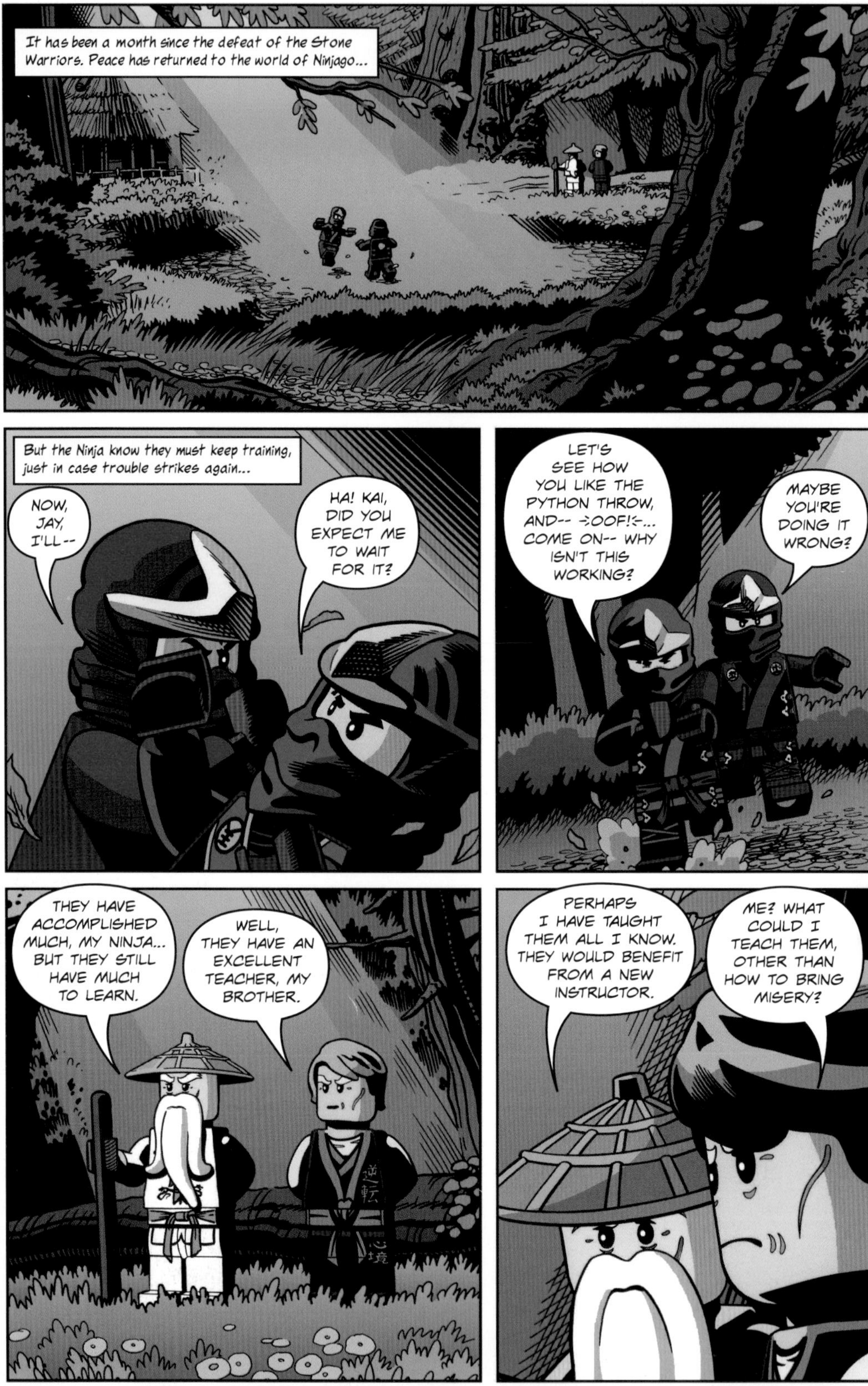
It has been a month since the defeat of the Stone Warriors. Peace has returned to the world of Ninjago...
But the Ninja know they must keep training, just in case trouble strikes again...
NOW, JAY, I'LL--
HA! KAI, DID YOU EXPECT ME TO WAIT FOR IT?
LET'S SEE HOW YOU LIKE THE PYTHON THROW, AND-- ⇒OOF!⇐... COME ON-- WHY ISN'T THIS WORKING?
MAYBE YOU'RE DOING IT WRONG?
THEY HAVE ACCOMPLISHED MUCH, MY NINJA... BUT THEY STILL HAVE MUCH TO LEARN.
WELL, THEY HAVE AN EXCELLENT TEACHER, MY BROTHER.
PERHAPS I HAVE TAUGHT THEM ALL I KNOW. THEY WOULD BENEFIT FROM A NEW INSTRUCTOR.
ME? WHAT COULD I TEACH THEM, OTHER THAN HOW TO BRING MISERY?

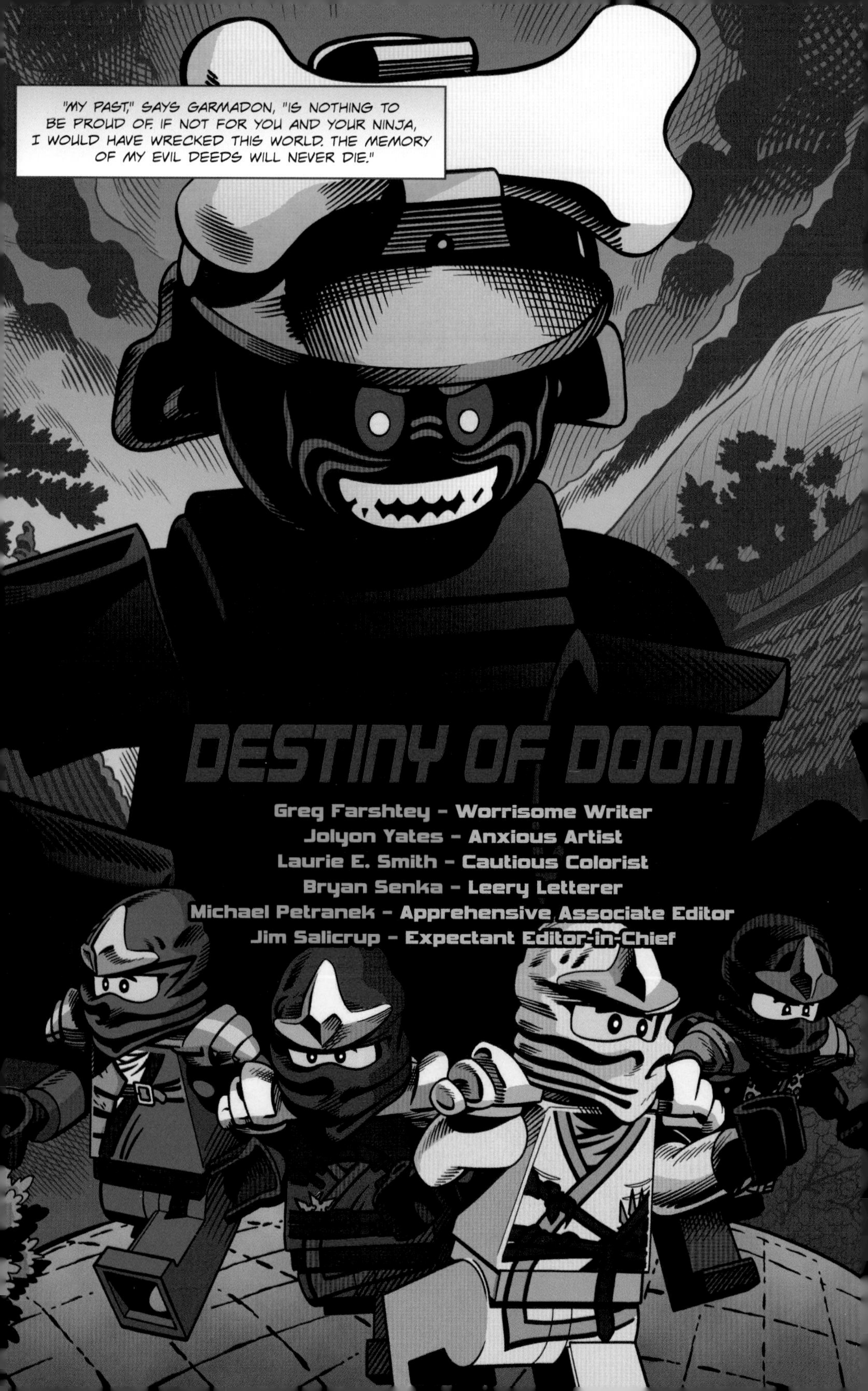
"MY PAST," SAYS GARMADON, "IS NOTHING TO BE PROUD OF. IF NOT FOR YOU AND YOUR NINJA, I WOULD HAVE WRECKED THIS WORLD. THE MEMORY OF MY EVIL DEEDS WILL NEVER DIE."
DESTINY OF DOOM
Greg Farshtey - Worrisome Writer
Jolyon Yates - Anxious Artist
Laurie E. Smith - Cautious Colorist
Bryan Senka - Leery Letterer
Michael Petranek - Apprehensive Associate Editor
Jim Salicrup - Expectant Editor-in-Chief

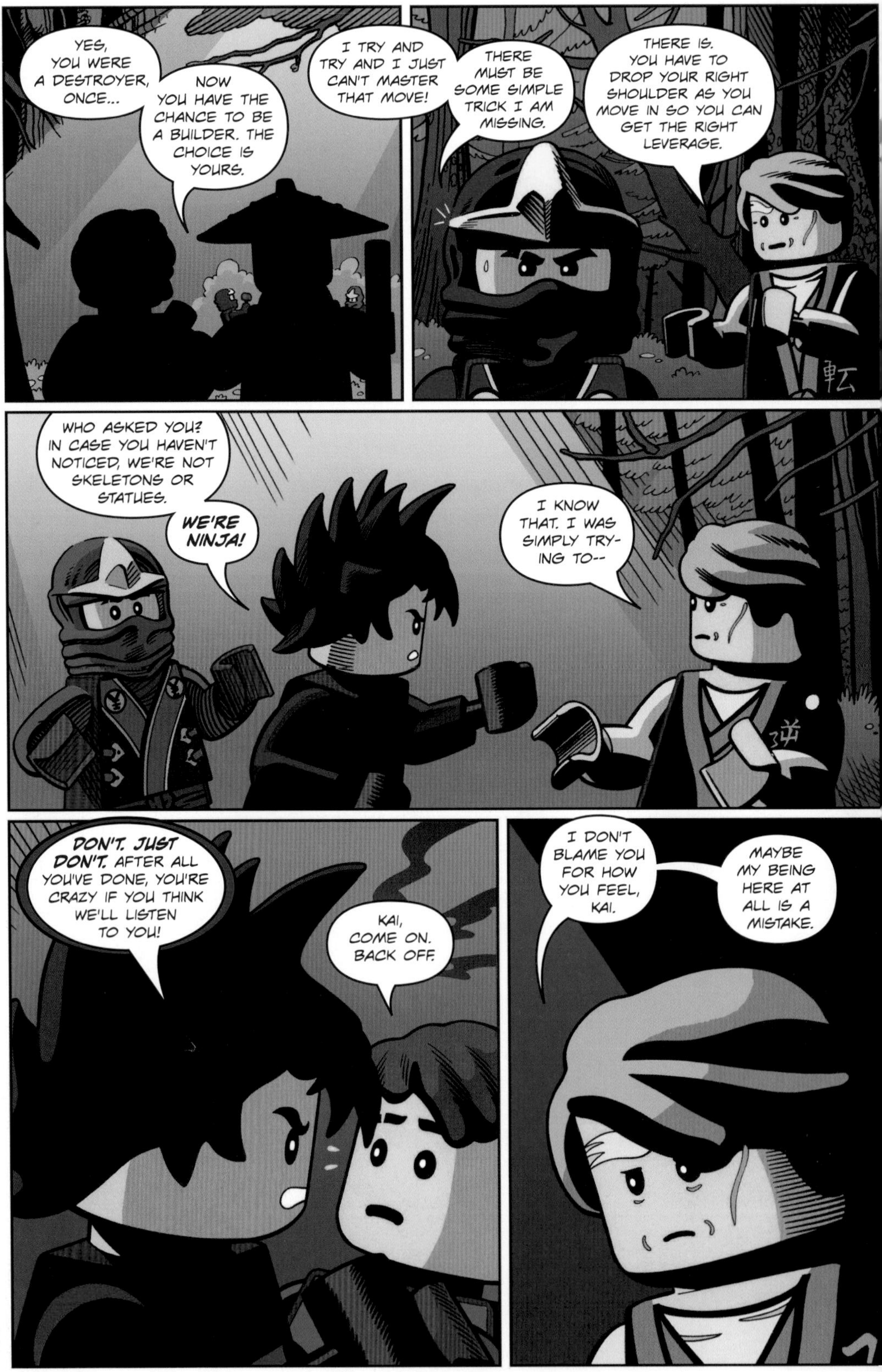

YES, YOU WERE A DESTROYER, ONCE...
NOW YOU HAVE THE CHANCE TO BE A BUILDER. THE CHOICE IS YOURS.
I TRY AND TRY AND I JUST CAN'T MASTER THAT MOVE!
THERE MUST BE SOME SIMPLE TRICK I AM MISSING.
THERE IS. YOU HAVE TO DROP YOUR RIGHT SHOULDER AS YOU MOVE IN SO YOU CAN GET THE RIGHT LEVERAGE.
WHO ASKED YOU? IN CASE YOU HAVEN'T NOTICED, WE'RE NOT SKELETONS OR STATUES.
WE'RE NINJA!
I KNOW THAT. I WAS SIMPLY TRY-ING TO--
DON'T. JUST DON'T. AFTER ALL YOU'VE DONE, YOU'RE CRAZY IF YOU THINK WE'LL LISTEN TO YOU!
KAI, COME ON. BACK OFF.
I DON'T BLAME YOU FOR HOW YOU FEEL, KAI.
MAYBE MY BEING HERE AT ALL IS A MISTAKE.

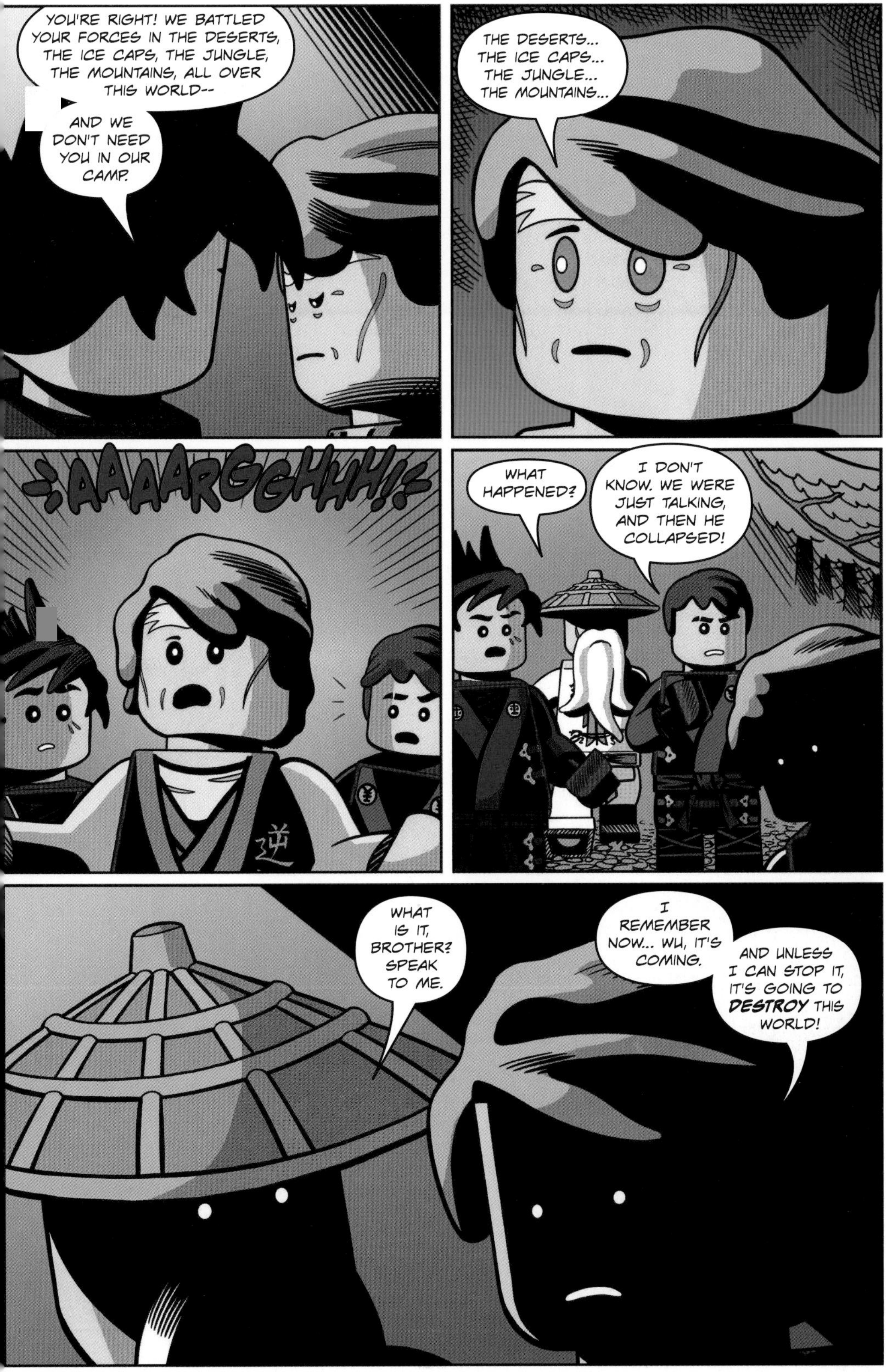

YOU'RE RIGHT! WE BATTLED YOUR FORCES IN THE DESERTS, THE ICE CAPS, THE JUNGLE, THE MOUNTAINS, ALL OVER THIS WORLD--
AND WE DON'T NEED YOU IN OUR CAMP.
THE DESERTS... THE ICE CAPS... THE JUNGLE... THE MOUNTAINS...
AAAARGGHHH!!
WHAT HAPPENED?
I DON'T KNOW. WE WERE JUST TALKING, AND THEN HE COLLAPSED!
WHAT IS IT, BROTHER? SPEAK TO ME.
I REMEMBER NOW... WU, IT'S COMING.
AND UNLESS I CAN STOP IT, IT'S GOING TO DESTROY THIS WORLD!

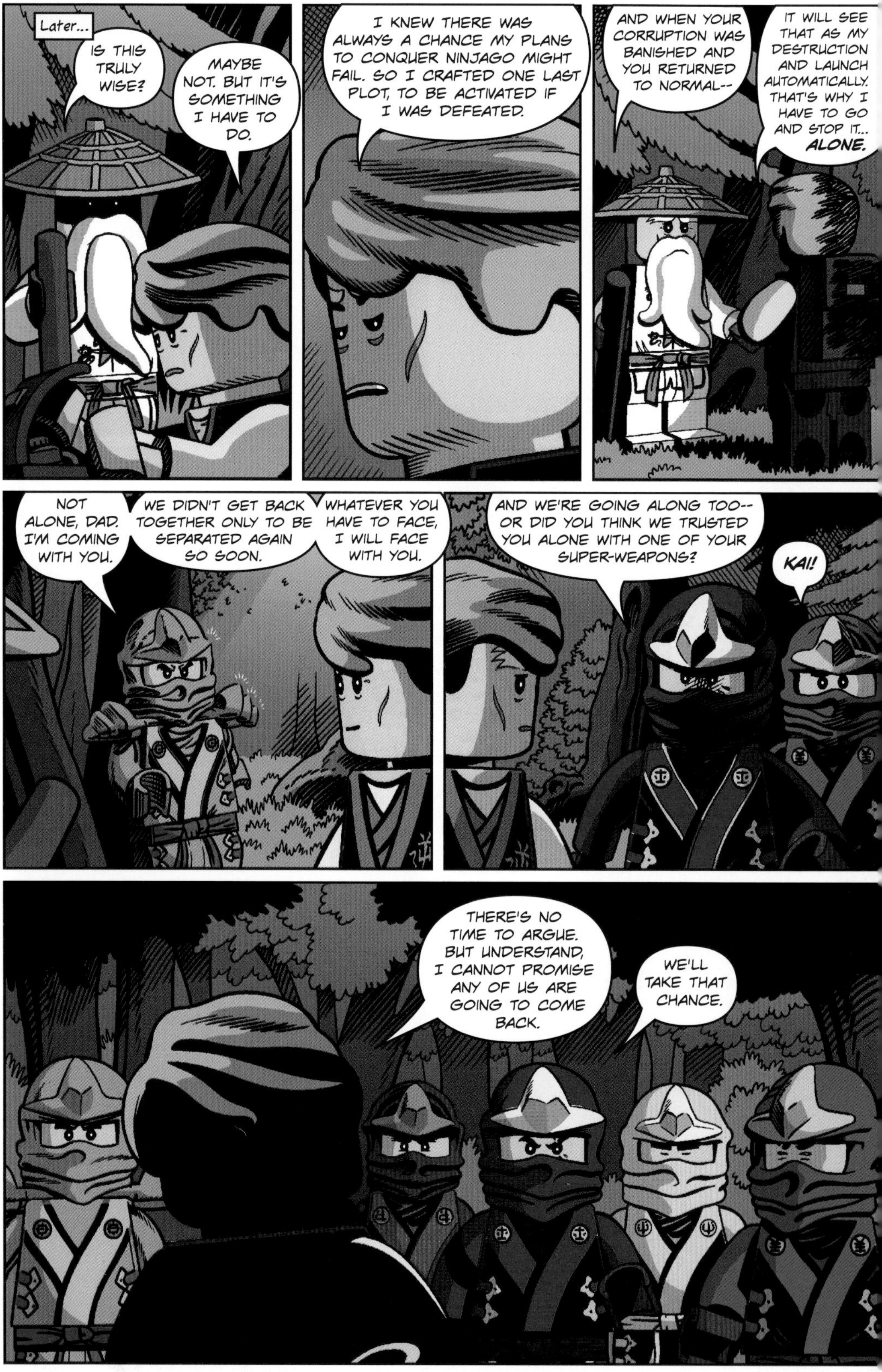
Later...
IS THIS TRULY WISE?
MAYBE NOT. BUT IT'S SOMETHING I HAVE TO DO.
I KNEW THERE WAS ALWAYS A CHANCE MY PLANS TO CONQUER NINJAGO MIGHT FAIL. SO I CRAFTED ONE LAST PLOT, TO BE ACTIVATED IF I WAS DEFEATED.
AND WHEN YOUR CORRUPTION WAS BANISHED AND YOU RETURNED TO NORMAL--
IT WILL SEE THAT AS MY DESTRUCTION AND LAUNCH AUTOMATICALLY. THAT'S WHY I HAVE TO GO AND STOP IT... ALONE.
NOT ALONE, DAD. I'M COMING WITH YOU.
WE DIDN'T GET BACK TOGETHER ONLY TO BE SEPARATED AGAIN SO SOON.
WHATEVER YOU HAVE TO FACE, I WILL FACE WITH YOU.
AND WE'RE GOING ALONG TOO-- OR DID YOU THINK WE TRUSTED YOU ALONE WITH ONE OF YOUR SUPER-WEAPONS?
KAI!
THERE'S NO TIME TO ARGUE. BUT UNDERSTAND, I CANNOT PROMISE ANY OF US ARE GOING TO COME BACK.
WE'LL TAKE THAT CHANCE.

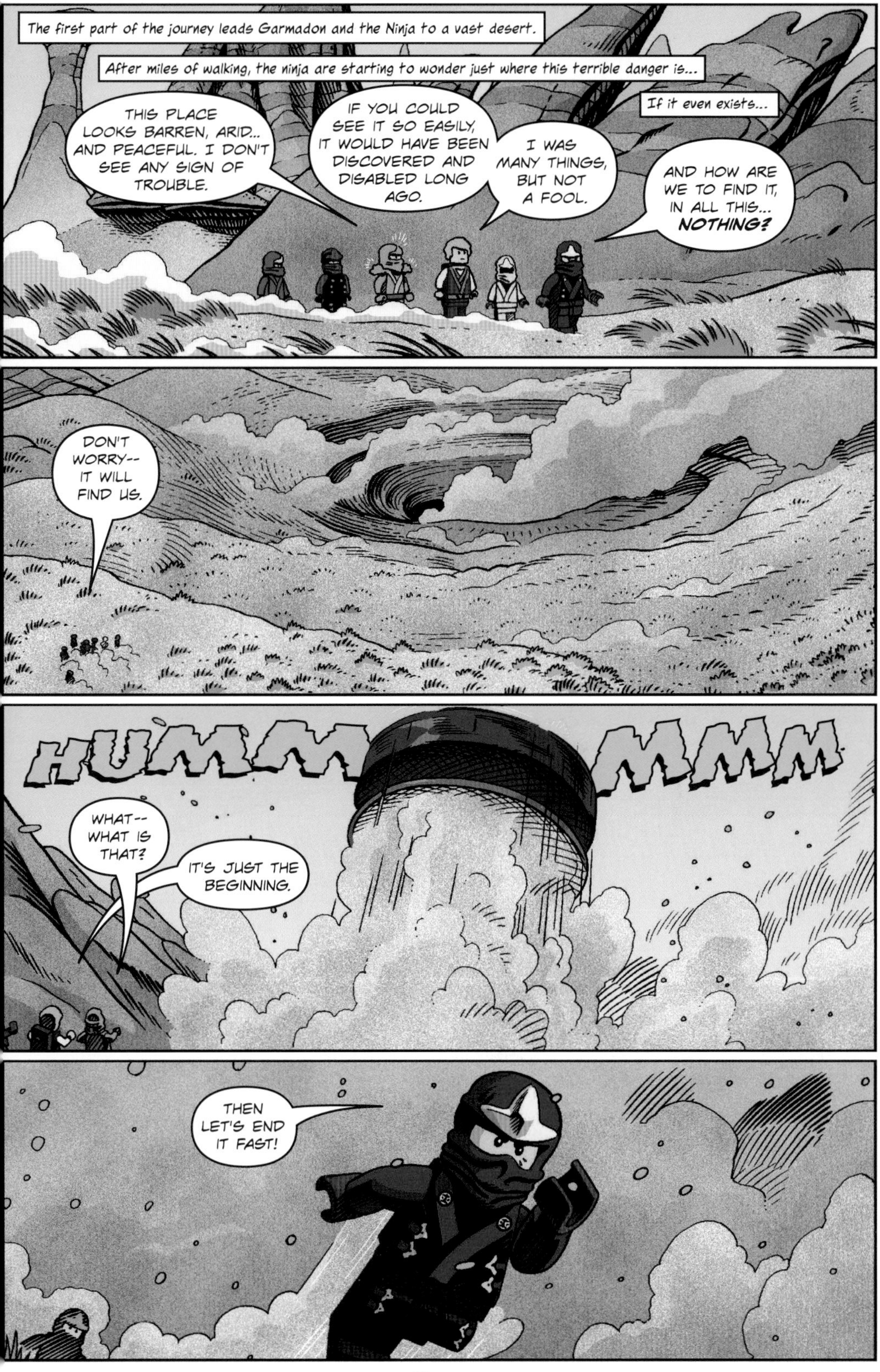
The first part of the journey leads Garmadon and the Ninja to a vast desert.
After miles of walking, the ninja are starting to wonder just where this terrible danger is...
THIS PLACE LOOKS BARREN, ARID... AND PEACEFUL. I DON'T SEE ANY SIGN OF TROUBLE.
IF YOU COULD SEE IT SO EASILY, IT WOULD HAVE BEEN DISCOVERED AND DISABLED LONG AGO.
I WAS MANY THINGS, BUT NOT A FOOL.
If it even exists...
AND HOW ARE WE TO FIND IT, IN ALL THIS... NOTHING?
DON'T WORRY-- IT WILL FIND US.
HUMMMMM
WHAT-- WHAT IS THAT?
IT'S JUST THE BEGINNING.
THEN LET'S END IT FAST!

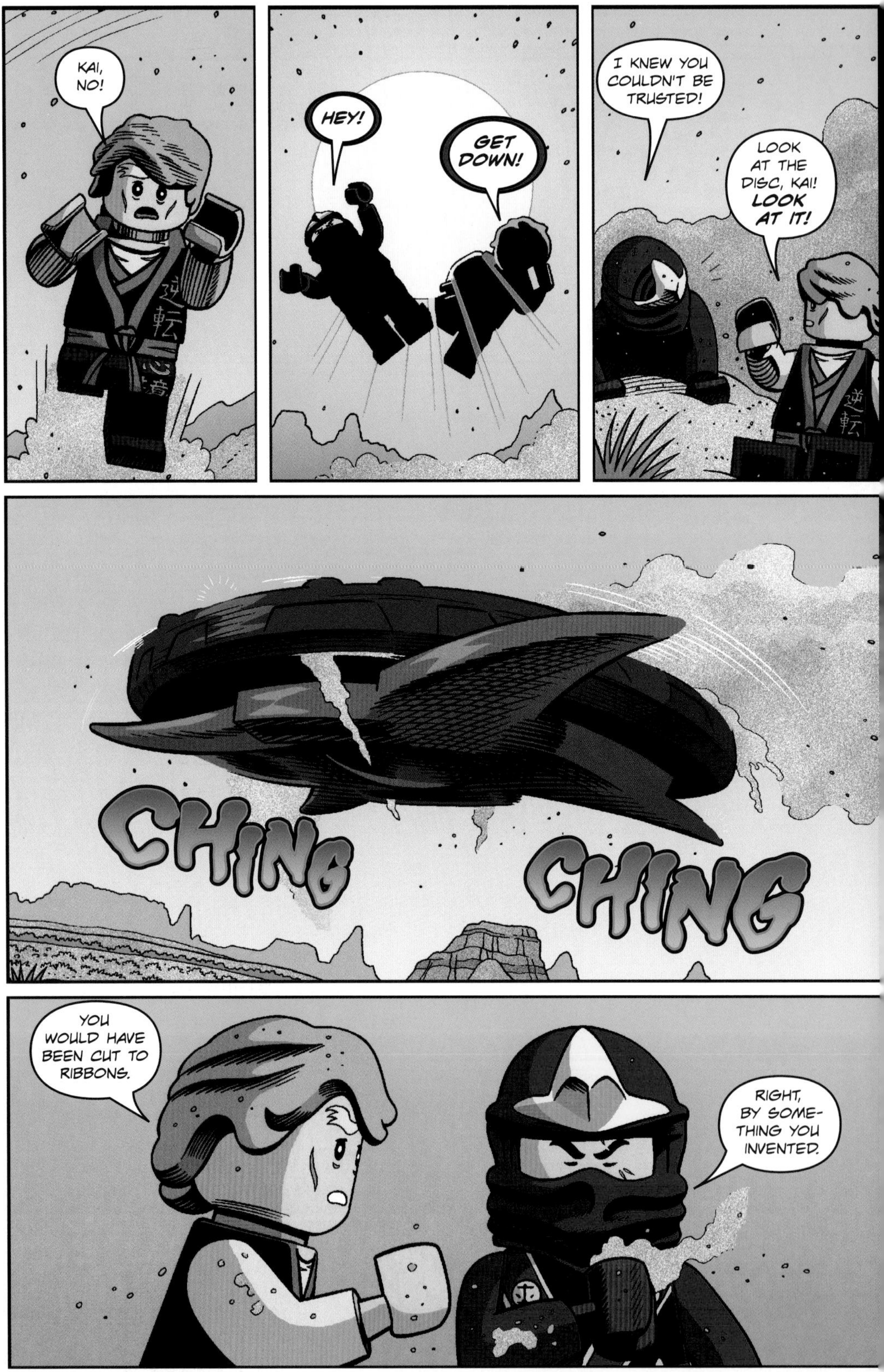
KAI, NO!
HEY!
GET DOWN!
I KNEW YOU COULDN'T BE TRUSTED!
LOOK AT THE DISC, KAI! **LOOK AT IT!**
CHING
CHING
YOU WOULD HAVE BEEN CUT TO RIBBONS.
RIGHT, BY SOME-THING YOU INVENTED.

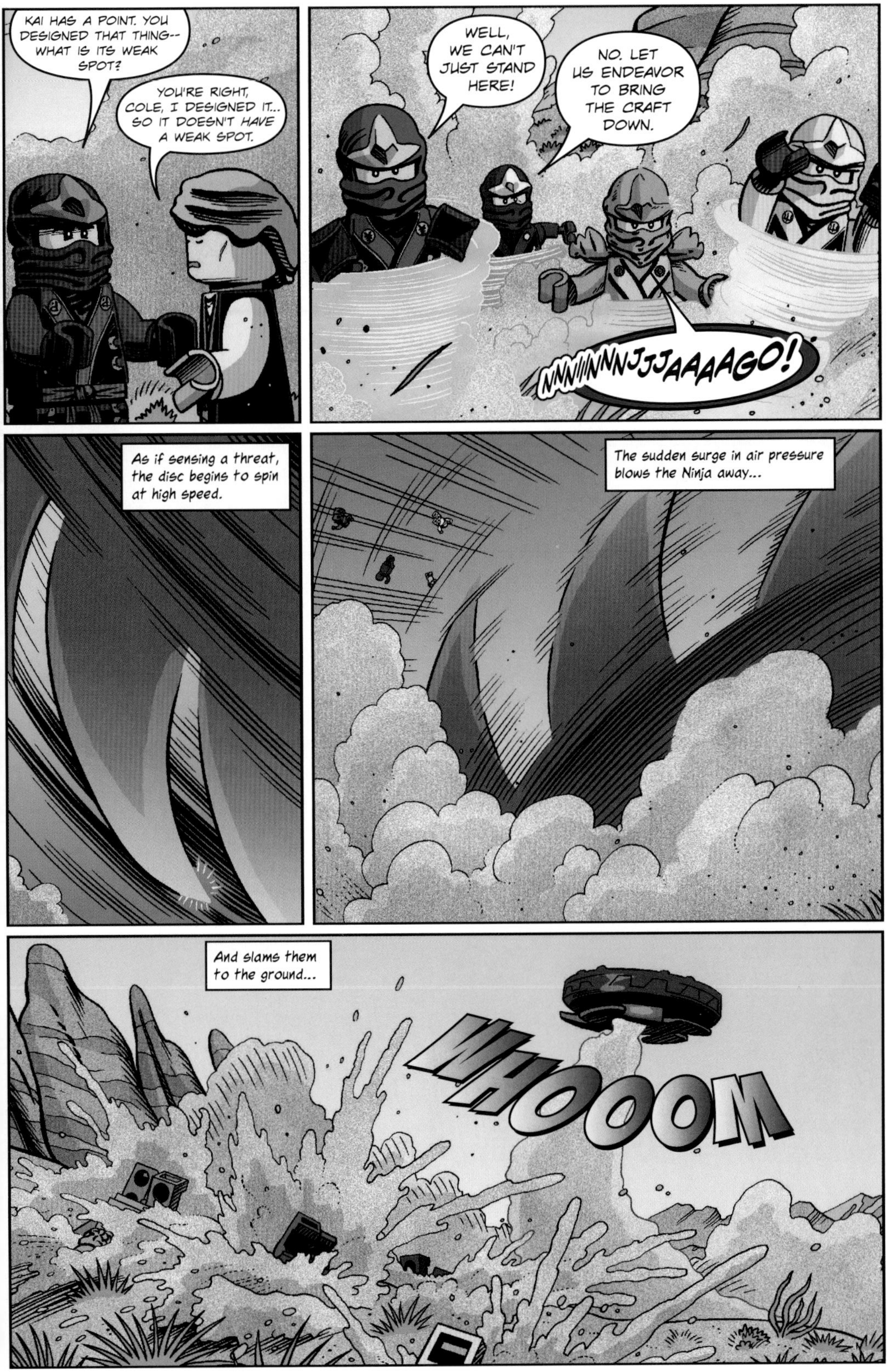
KAI HAS A POINT. YOU DESIGNED THAT THING-- WHAT IS ITS WEAK SPOT?
YOU'RE RIGHT, COLE, I DESIGNED IT... SO IT DOESN'T HAVE A WEAK SPOT.
WELL, WE CAN'T JUST STAND HERE!
NO. LET US ENDEAVOR TO BRING THE CRAFT DOWN.
NNNNNNJJAAAAGO!
As if sensing a threat, the disc begins to spin at high speed.
The sudden surge in air pressure blows the Ninja away...
And slams them to the ground...
WHOOOM

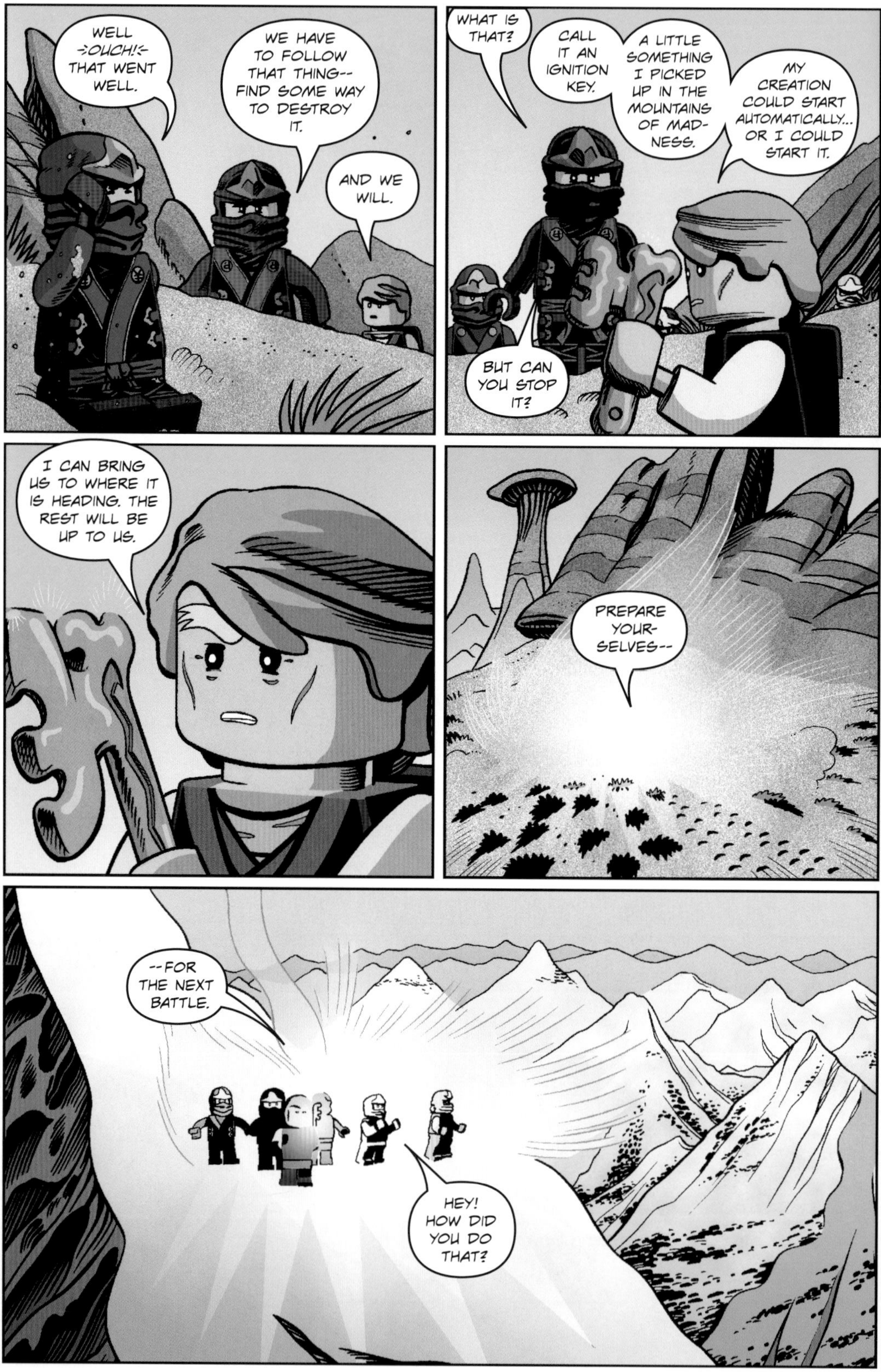

WELL →OUCH!← THAT WENT WELL.
WE HAVE TO FOLLOW THAT THING-- FIND SOME WAY TO DESTROY IT.
AND WE WILL.
WHAT IS THAT?
CALL IT AN IGNITION KEY.
A LITTLE SOMETHING I PICKED UP IN THE MOUNTAINS OF MAD-NESS.
MY CREATION COULD START AUTOMATICALLY... OR I COULD START IT.
BUT CAN YOU STOP IT?
I CAN BRING US TO WHERE IT IS HEADING. THE REST WILL BE UP TO US.
PREPARE YOUR-SELVES--
--FOR THE NEXT BATTLE.
HEY! HOW DID YOU DO THAT?

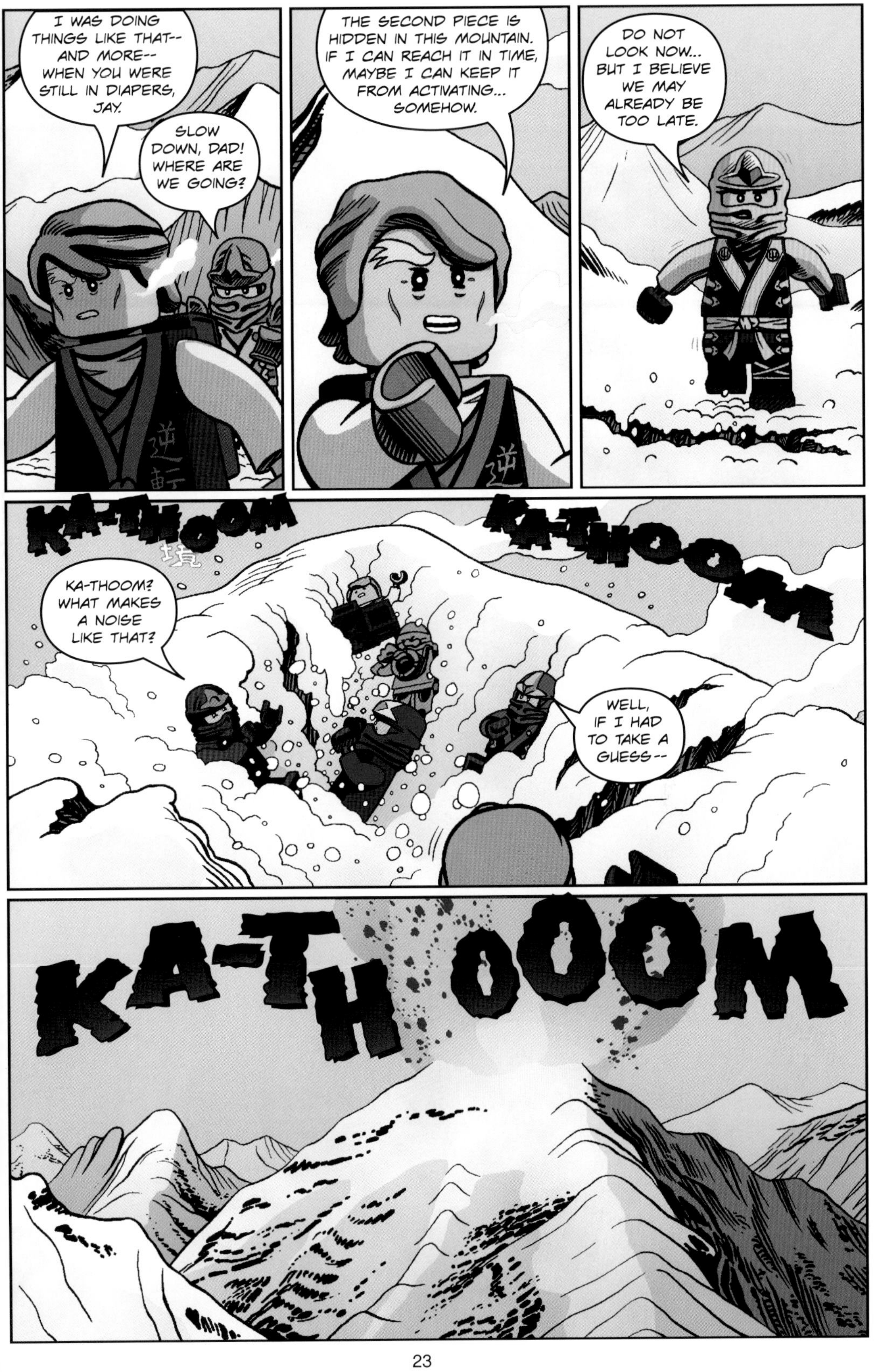
I WAS DOING THINGS LIKE THAT-- AND MORE-- WHEN YOU WERE STILL IN DIAPERS, JAY.
SLOW DOWN, DAD! WHERE ARE WE GOING?
THE SECOND PIECE IS HIDDEN IN THIS MOUNTAIN. IF I CAN REACH IT IN TIME, MAYBE I CAN KEEP IT FROM ACTIVATING... SOMEHOW.
DO NOT LOOK NOW... BUT I BELIEVE WE MAY ALREADY BE TOO LATE.
KA-THOOM
KA-THOOOM
KA-THOOM? WHAT MAKES A NOISE LIKE THAT?
WELL, IF I HAD TO TAKE A GUESS--
KA-THOOOM

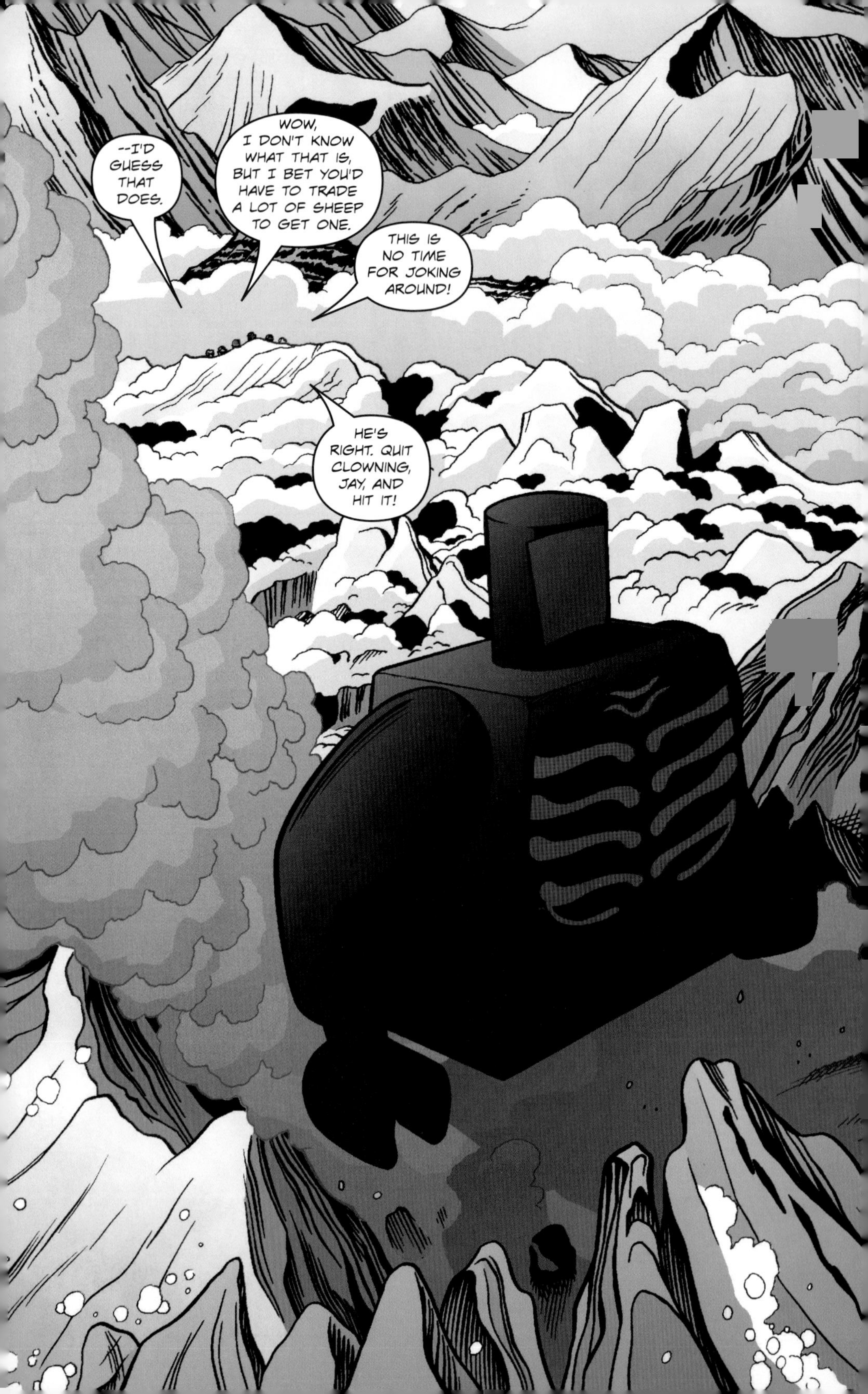
WOW, I DON'T KNOW WHAT THAT IS, BUT I BET YOU'D HAVE TO TRADE A LOT OF SHEEP TO GET ONE.
--I'D GUESS THAT DOES.
THIS IS NO TIME FOR JOKING AROUND!
HE'S RIGHT. QUIT CLOWNING, JAY, AND HIT IT!

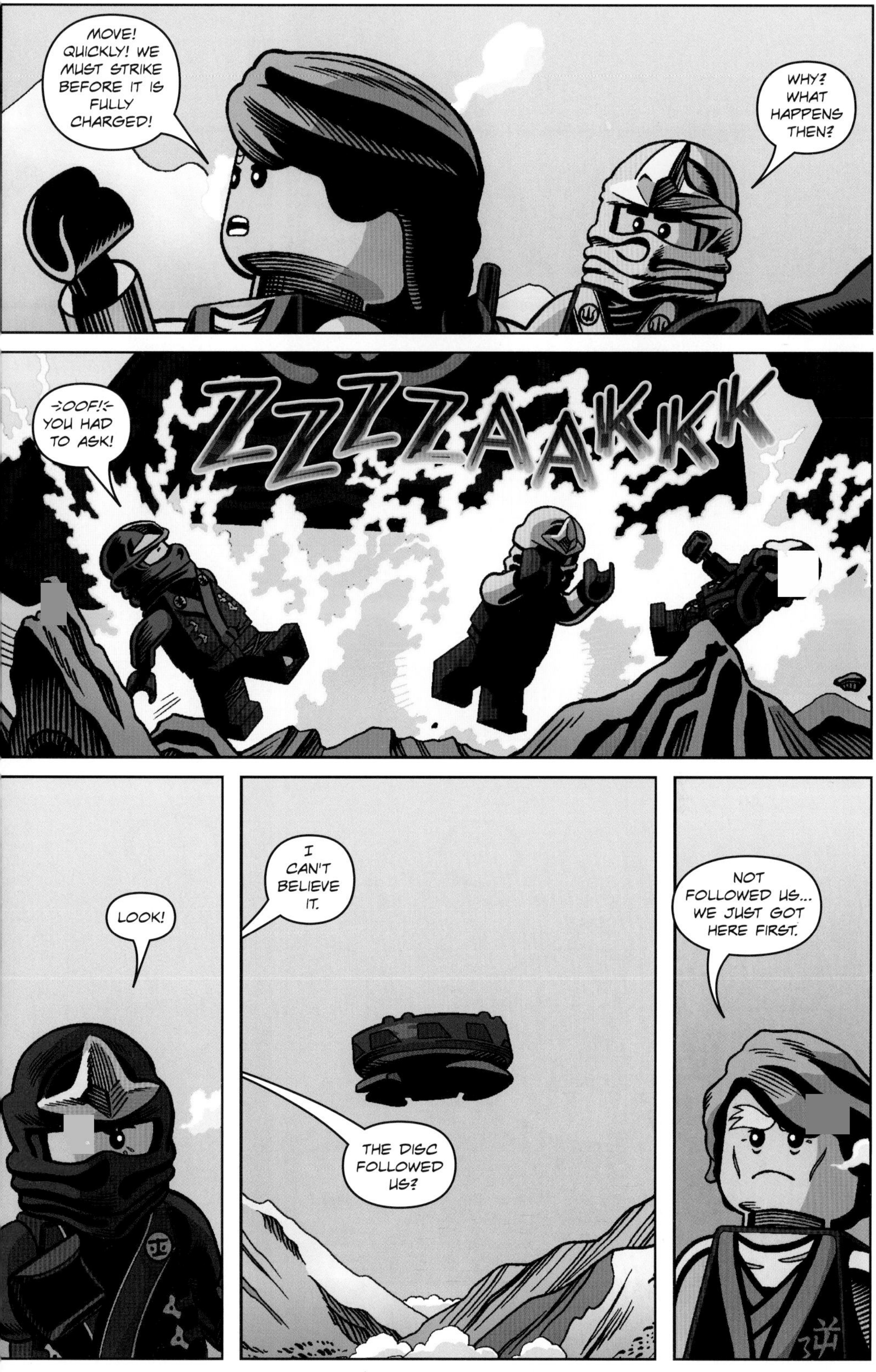
MOVE! QUICKLY! WE MUST STRIKE BEFORE IT IS FULLY CHARGED!
WHY? WHAT HAPPENS THEN?
ZZZZAAKKK
-OOF!- YOU HAD TO ASK!
LOOK!
I CAN'T BELIEVE IT.
THE DISC FOLLOWED US?
NOT FOLLOWED US... WE JUST GOT HERE FIRST.

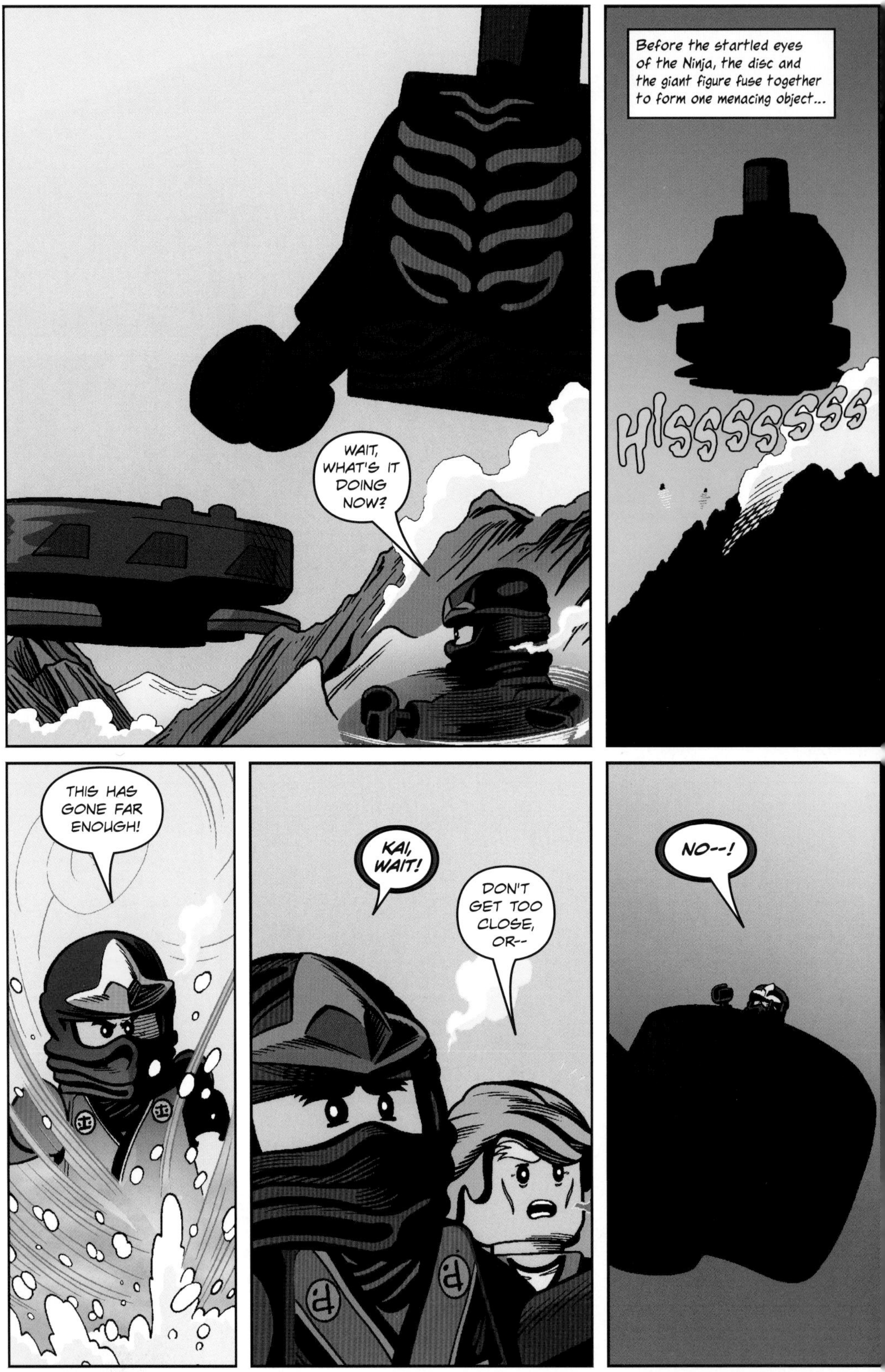
WAIT, WHAT'S IT DOING NOW?
Before the startled eyes of the Ninja, the disc and the giant figure fuse together to form one menacing object...
HISSSSSSS
THIS HAS GONE FAR ENOUGH!
KAI, WAIT!
DON'T GET TOO CLOSE, OR--
NO--!

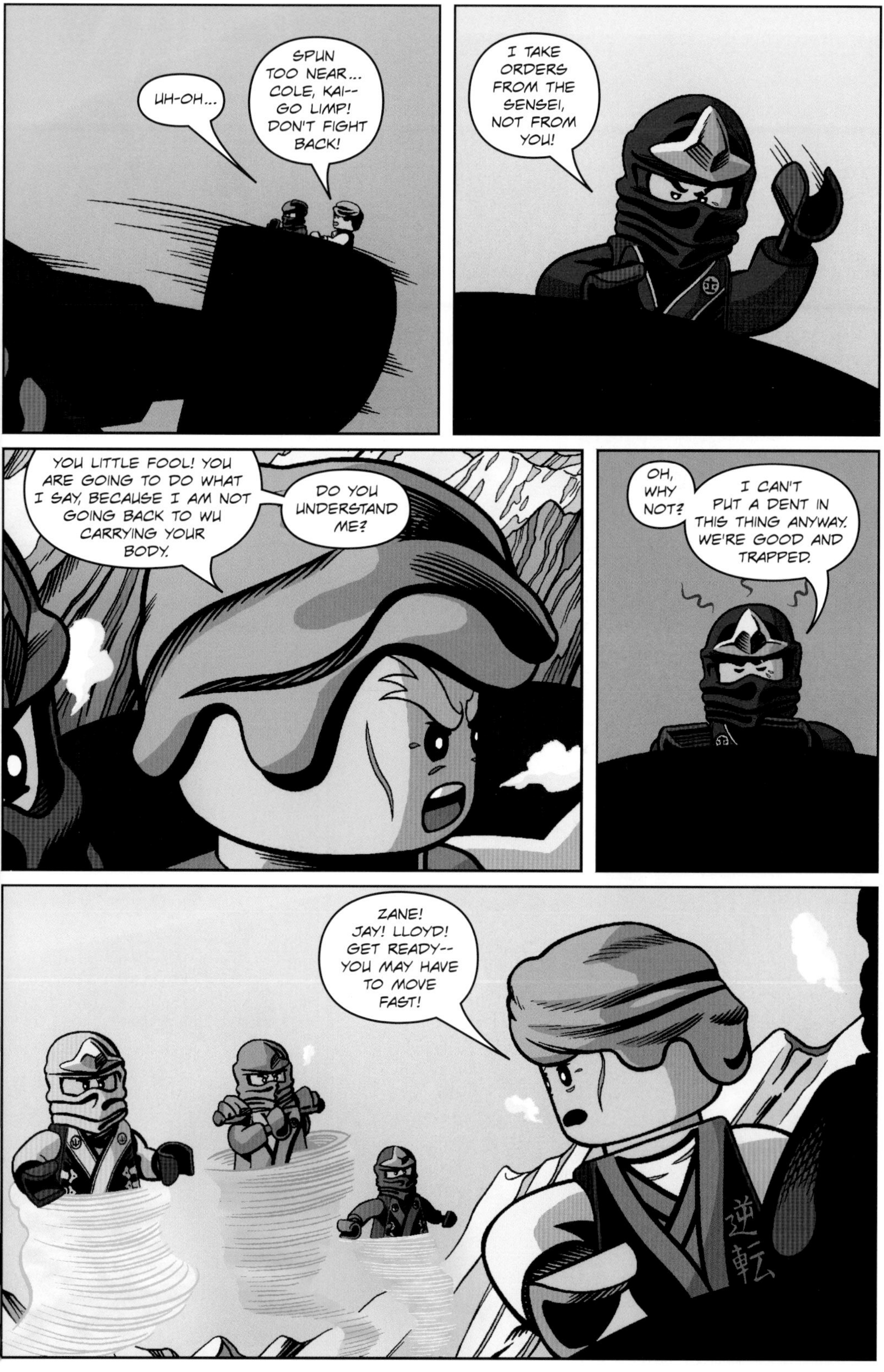
UH-OH...
SPUN TOO NEAR... COLE, KAI-- GO LIMP! DON'T FIGHT BACK!
I TAKE ORDERS FROM THE SENSEI, NOT FROM YOU!
YOU LITTLE FOOL! YOU ARE GOING TO DO WHAT I SAY, BECAUSE I AM NOT GOING BACK TO WU CARRYING YOUR BODY.
DO YOU UNDERSTAND ME?
OH, WHY NOT?
I CAN'T PUT A DENT IN THIS THING ANYWAY. WE'RE GOOD AND TRAPPED.
ZANE! JAY! LLOYD! GET READY-- YOU MAY HAVE TO MOVE FAST!
逆転

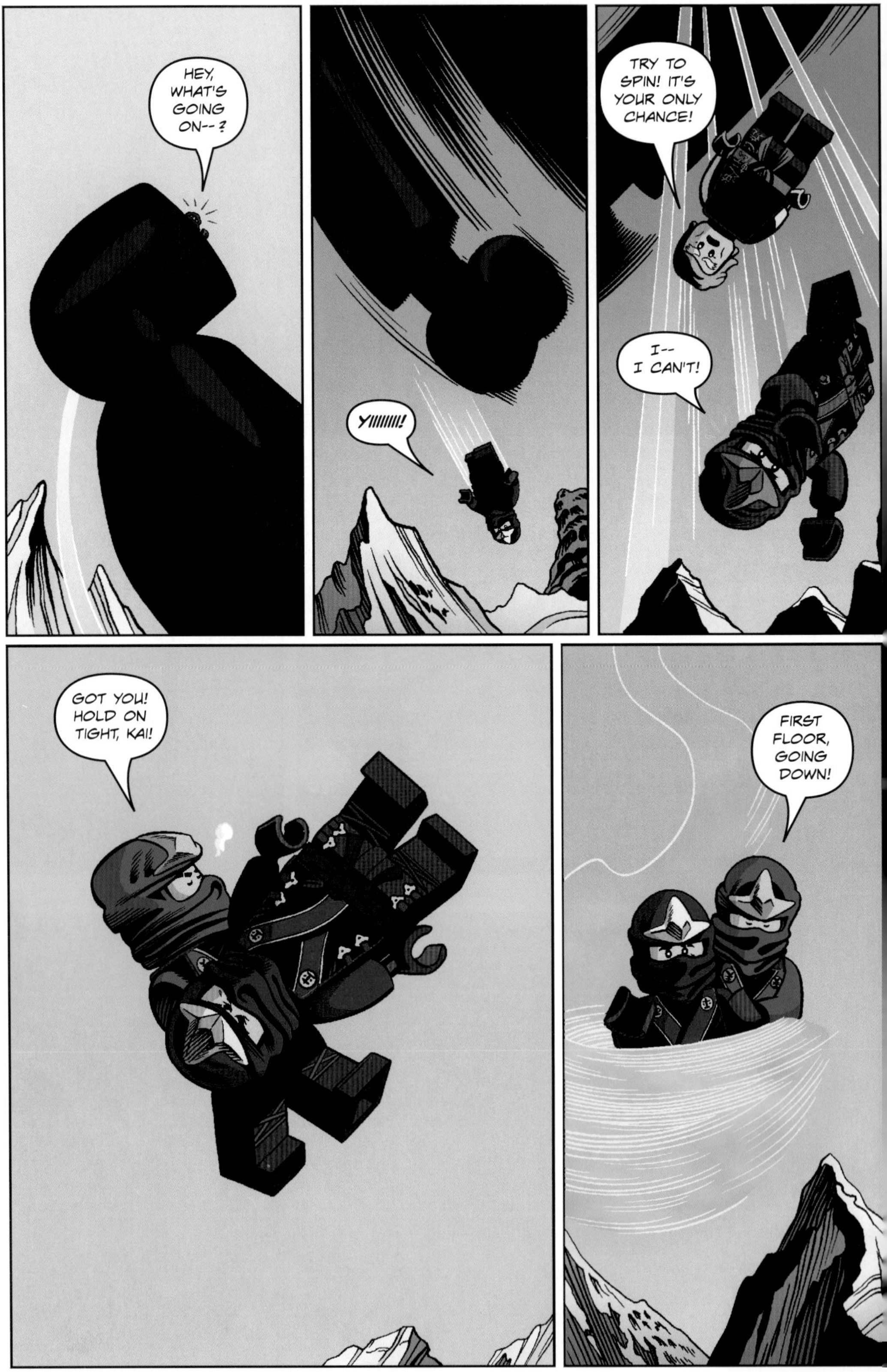
HEY, WHAT'S GOING ON--?
YIIIIIII!
TRY TO SPIN! IT'S YOUR ONLY CHANCE!
I-- I CAN'T!
GOT YOU! HOLD ON TIGHT, KAI!
FIRST FLOOR, GOING DOWN!

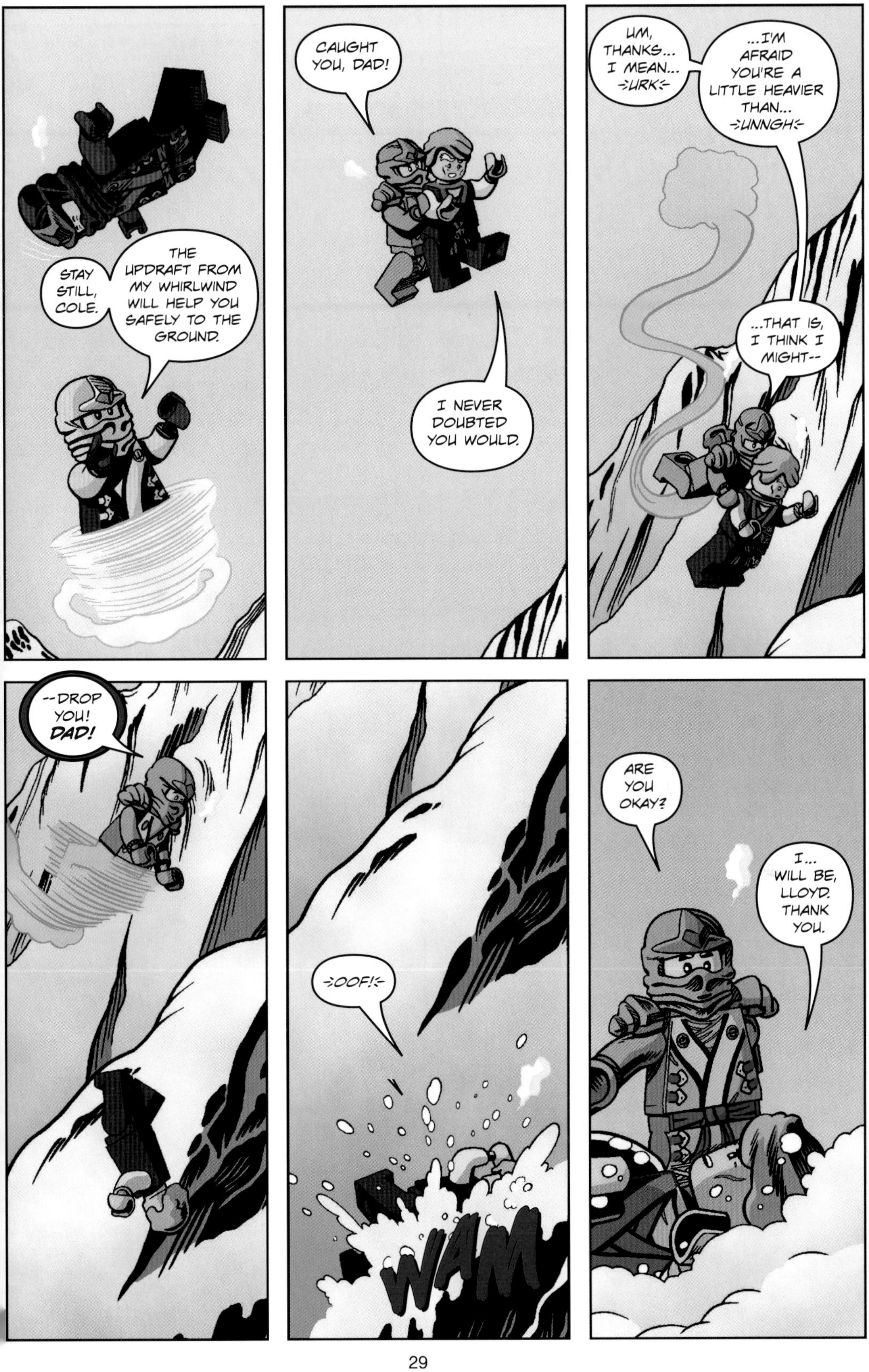
STAY STILL, COLE.
THE UPDRAFT FROM MY WHIRLWIND WILL HELP YOU SAFELY TO THE GROUND.
CAUGHT YOU, DAD!
I NEVER DOUBTED YOU WOULD.
UM, THANKS... I MEAN... URK
...I'M AFRAID YOU'RE A LITTLE HEAVIER THAN... UNNGH
...THAT IS, I THINK I MIGHT--
--DROP YOU! DAD!
OOF!
WAM
ARE YOU OKAY?
I... WILL BE, LLOYD. THANK YOU.

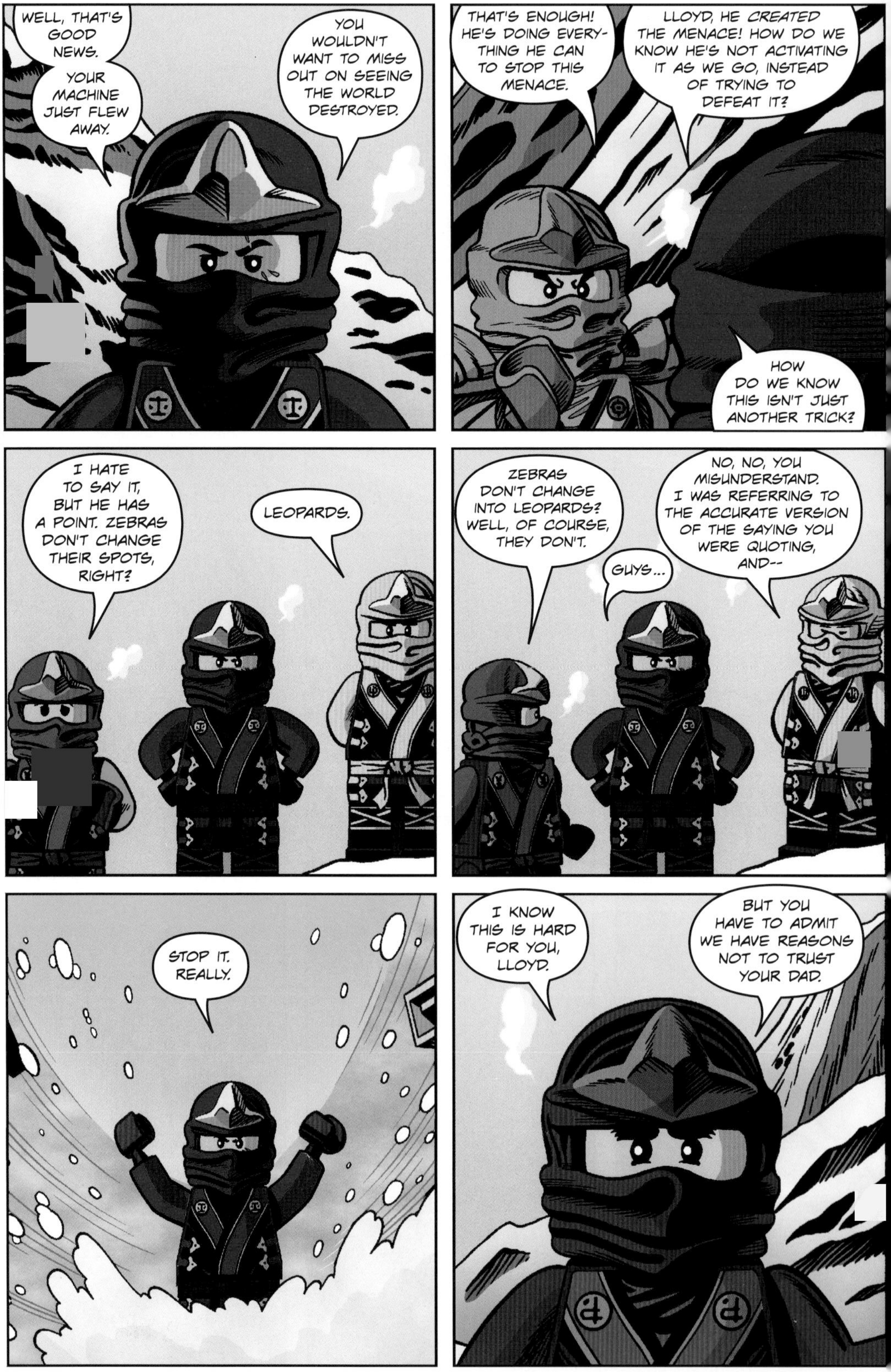
WELL, THAT'S GOOD NEWS.
YOUR MACHINE JUST FLEW AWAY.
YOU WOULDN'T WANT TO MISS OUT ON SEEING THE WORLD DESTROYED.
THAT'S ENOUGH! HE'S DOING EVERY-THING HE CAN TO STOP THIS MENACE.
LLOYD, HE CREATED THE MENACE! HOW DO WE KNOW HE'S NOT ACTIVATING IT AS WE GO, INSTEAD OF TRYING TO DEFEAT IT?
HOW DO WE KNOW THIS ISN'T JUST ANOTHER TRICK?
I HATE TO SAY IT, BUT HE HAS A POINT. ZEBRAS DON'T CHANGE THEIR SPOTS, RIGHT?
LEOPARDS.
ZEBRAS DON'T CHANGE INTO LEOPARDS? WELL, OF COURSE, THEY DON'T.
NO, NO, YOU MISUNDERSTAND. I WAS REFERRING TO THE ACCURATE VERSION OF THE SAYING YOU WERE QUOTING, AND--
GUYS...
STOP IT. REALLY.
I KNOW THIS IS HARD FOR YOU, LLOYD.
BUT YOU HAVE TO ADMIT WE HAVE REASONS NOT TO TRUST YOUR DAD.

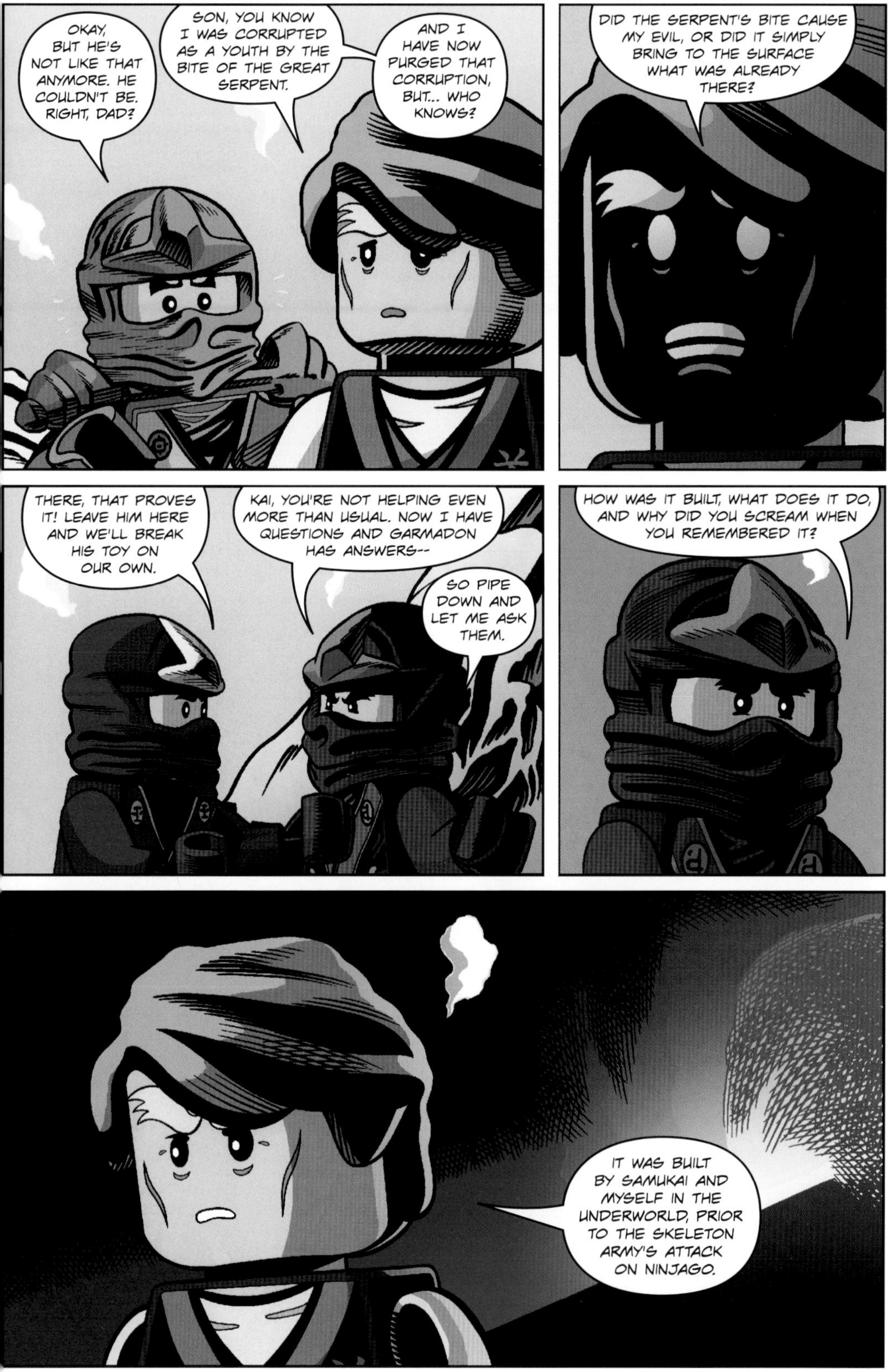

OKAY, BUT HE'S NOT LIKE THAT ANYMORE. HE COULDN'T BE. RIGHT, DAD?
SON, YOU KNOW I WAS CORRUPTED AS A YOUTH BY THE BITE OF THE GREAT SERPENT.
AND I HAVE NOW PURGED THAT CORRUPTION, BUT... WHO KNOWS?
DID THE SERPENT'S BITE CAUSE MY EVIL, OR DID IT SIMPLY BRING TO THE SURFACE WHAT WAS ALREADY THERE?
THERE, THAT PROVES IT! LEAVE HIM HERE AND WE'LL BREAK HIS TOY ON OUR OWN.
KAI, YOU'RE NOT HELPING EVEN MORE THAN USUAL. NOW I HAVE QUESTIONS AND GARMADON HAS ANSWERS--
SO PIPE DOWN AND LET ME ASK THEM.
HOW WAS IT BUILT, WHAT DOES IT DO, AND WHY DID YOU SCREAM WHEN YOU REMEMBERED IT?
IT WAS BUILT BY SAMUKAI AND MYSELF IN THE UNDERWORLD, PRIOR TO THE SKELETON ARMY'S ATTACK ON NINJAGO.

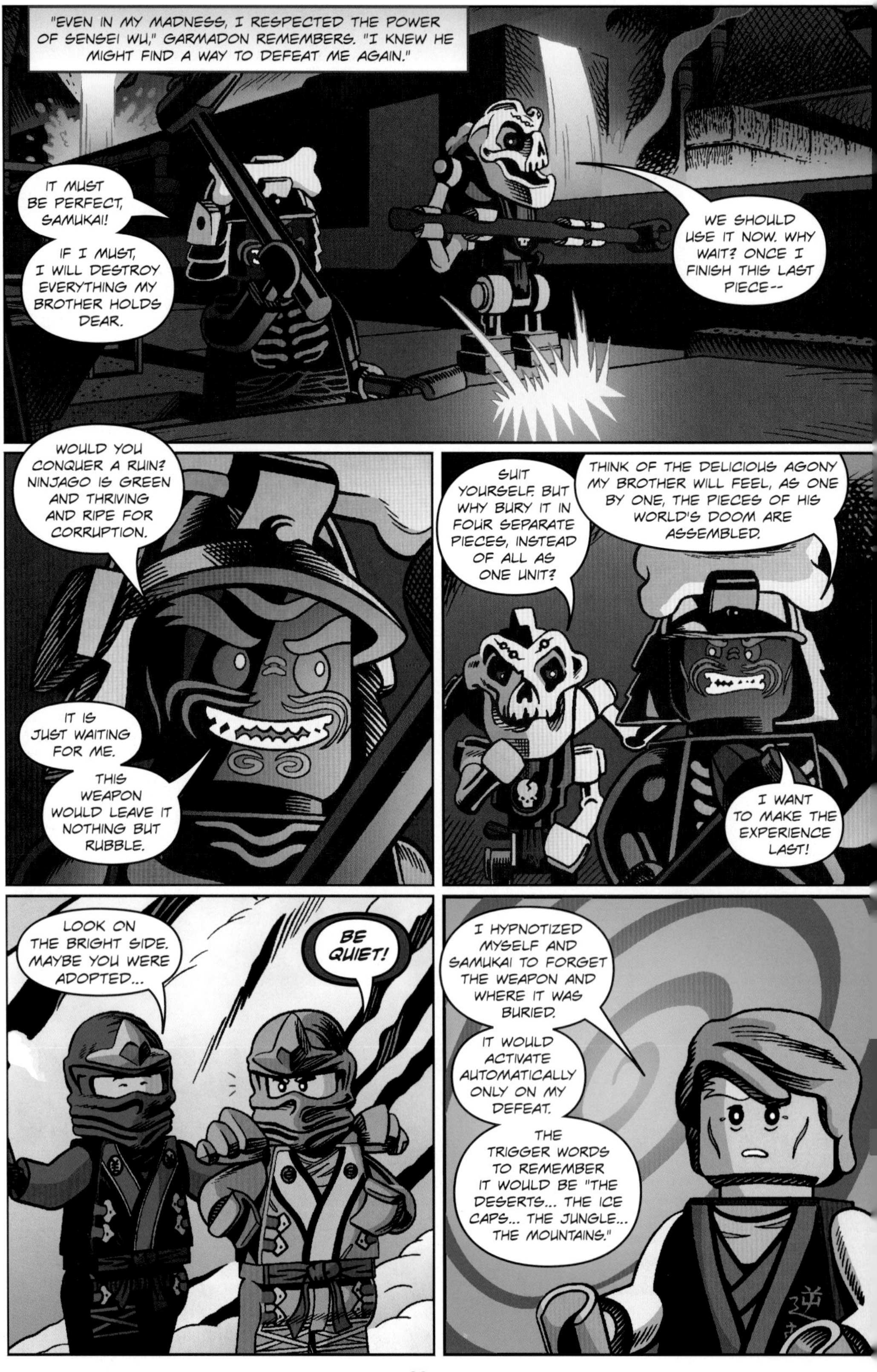
"EVEN IN MY MADNESS, I RESPECTED THE POWER OF SENSEI WU," GARMADON REMEMBERS. "I KNEW HE MIGHT FIND A WAY TO DEFEAT ME AGAIN."
IT MUST BE PERFECT, SAMUKAI!
IF I MUST, I WILL DESTROY EVERYTHING MY BROTHER HOLDS DEAR.
WE SHOULD USE IT NOW. WHY WAIT? ONCE I FINISH THIS LAST PIECE--
WOULD YOU CONQUER A RUIN? NINJAGO IS GREEN AND THRIVING AND RIPE FOR CORRUPTION.
IT IS JUST WAITING FOR ME.
THIS WEAPON WOULD LEAVE IT NOTHING BUT RUBBLE.
SUIT YOURSELF. BUT WHY BURY IT IN FOUR SEPARATE PIECES, INSTEAD OF ALL AS ONE UNIT?
THINK OF THE DELICIOUS AGONY MY BROTHER WILL FEEL, AS ONE BY ONE, THE PIECES OF HIS WORLD'S DOOM ARE ASSEMBLED.
I WANT TO MAKE THE EXPERIENCE LAST!
LOOK ON THE BRIGHT SIDE. MAYBE YOU WERE ADOPTED...
BE QUIET!
I HYPNOTIZED MYSELF AND SAMUKAI TO FORGET THE WEAPON AND WHERE IT WAS BURIED.
IT WOULD ACTIVATE AUTOMATICALLY ONLY ON MY DEFEAT.
THE TRIGGER WORDS TO REMEMBER IT WOULD BE "THE DESERTS... THE ICE CAPS... THE JUNGLE... THE MOUNTAINS."

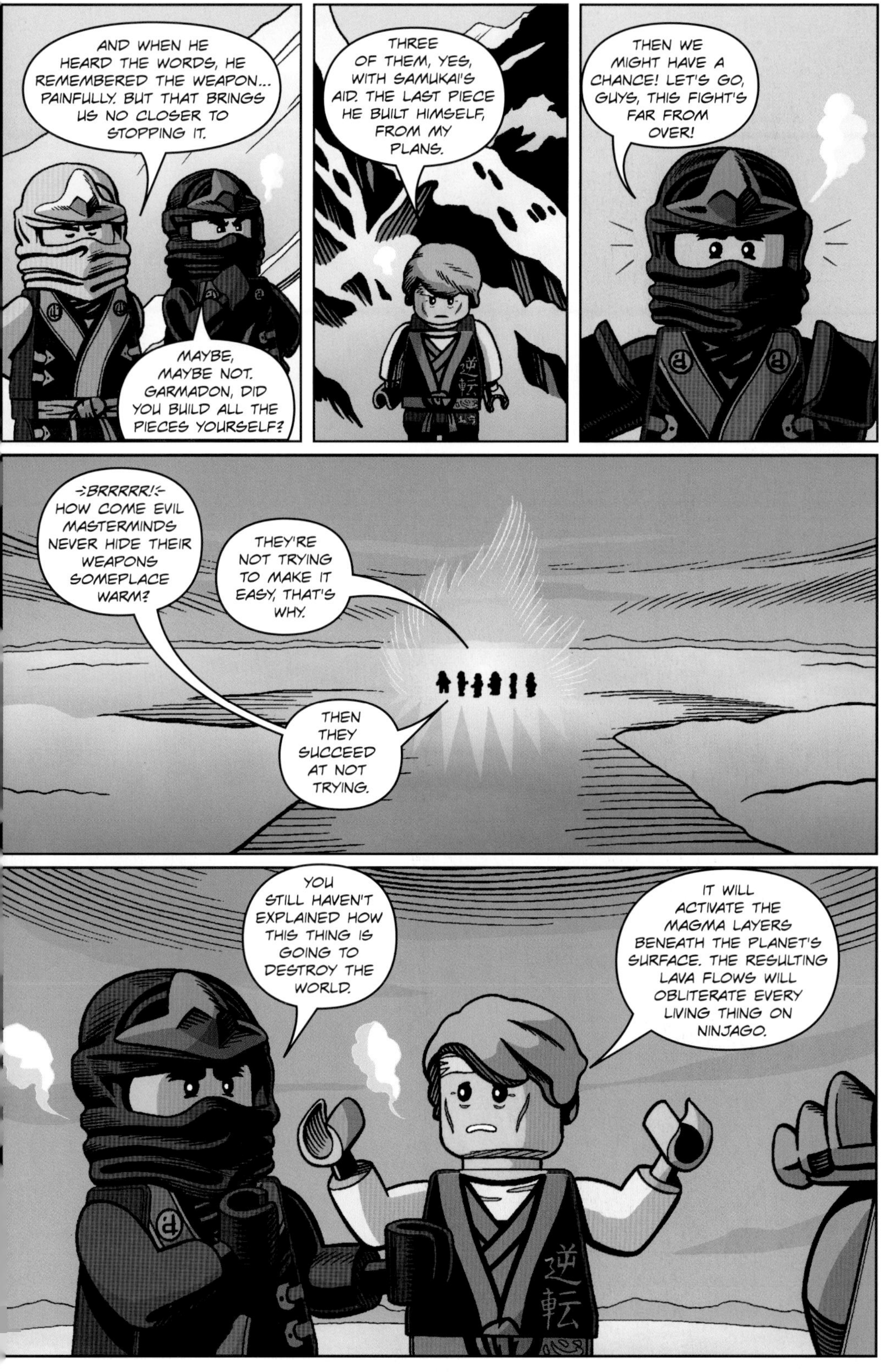
AND WHEN HE HEARD THE WORDS, HE REMEMBERED THE WEAPON... PAINFULLY. BUT THAT BRINGS US NO CLOSER TO STOPPING IT.
MAYBE, MAYBE NOT. GARMADON, DID YOU BUILD ALL THE PIECES YOURSELF?
THREE OF THEM, YES, WITH SAMUKAI'S AID. THE LAST PIECE HE BUILT HIMSELF, FROM MY PLANS.
THEN WE MIGHT HAVE A CHANCE! LET'S GO, GUYS, THIS FIGHT'S FAR FROM OVER!
BRRRRR! HOW COME EVIL MASTERMINDS NEVER HIDE THEIR WEAPONS SOMEPLACE WARM?
THEY'RE NOT TRYING TO MAKE IT EASY, THAT'S WHY.
THEN THEY SUCCEED AT NOT TRYING.
YOU STILL HAVEN'T EXPLAINED HOW THIS THING IS GOING TO DESTROY THE WORLD.
IT WILL ACTIVATE THE MAGMA LAYERS BENEATH THE PLANET'S SURFACE. THE RESULTING LAVA FLOWS WILL OBLITERATE EVERY LIVING THING ON NINJAGO.

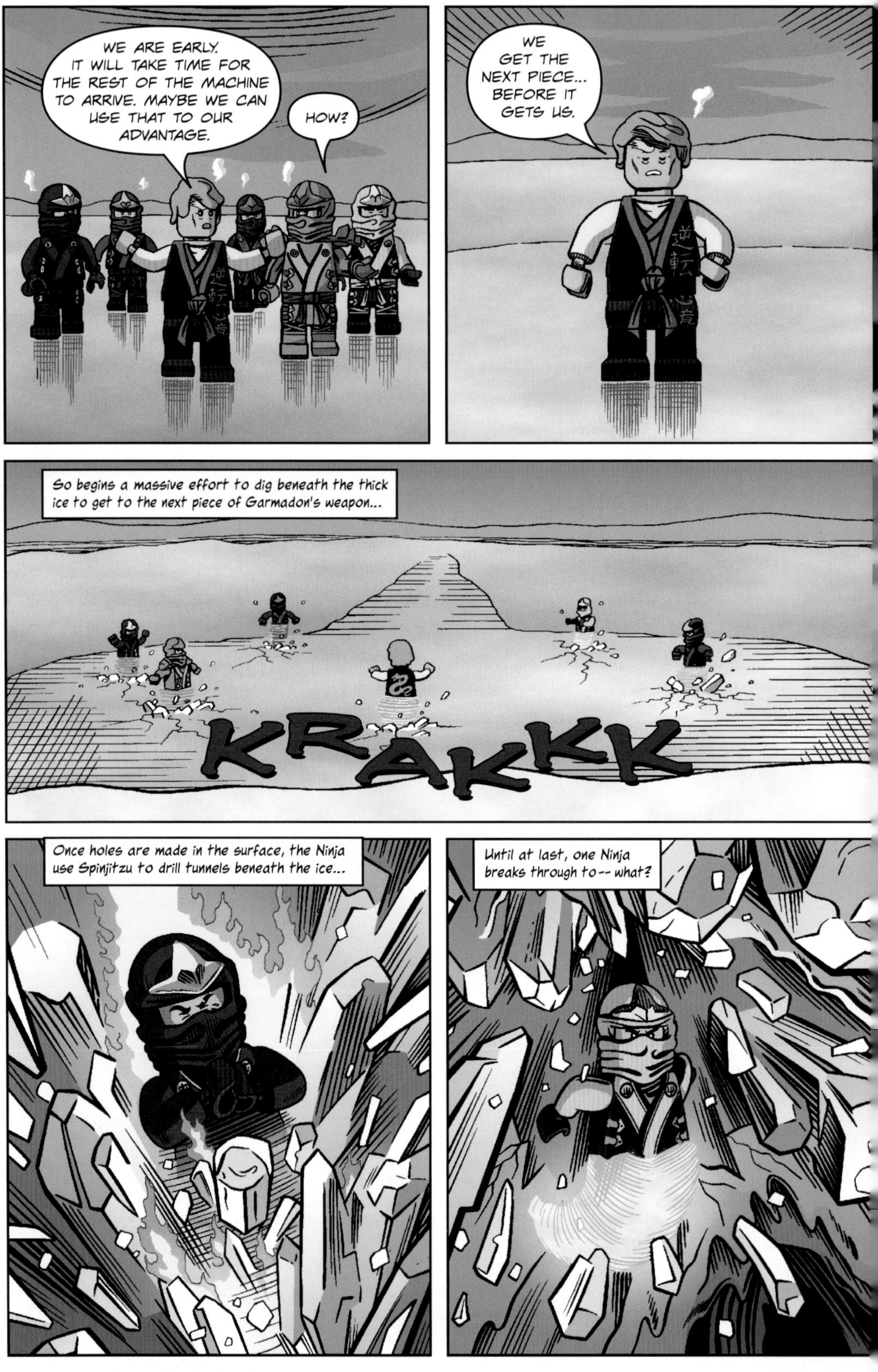
WE ARE EARLY. IT WILL TAKE TIME FOR THE REST OF THE MACHINE TO ARRIVE. MAYBE WE CAN USE THAT TO OUR ADVANTAGE.
HOW?
WE GET THE NEXT PIECE... BEFORE IT GETS US.
So begins a massive effort to dig beneath the thick ice to get to the next piece of Garmadon's weapon...
KRAKKK
Once holes are made in the surface, the Ninja use Spinjitzu to drill tunnels beneath the ice...
Until at last, one Ninja breaks through to-- what?

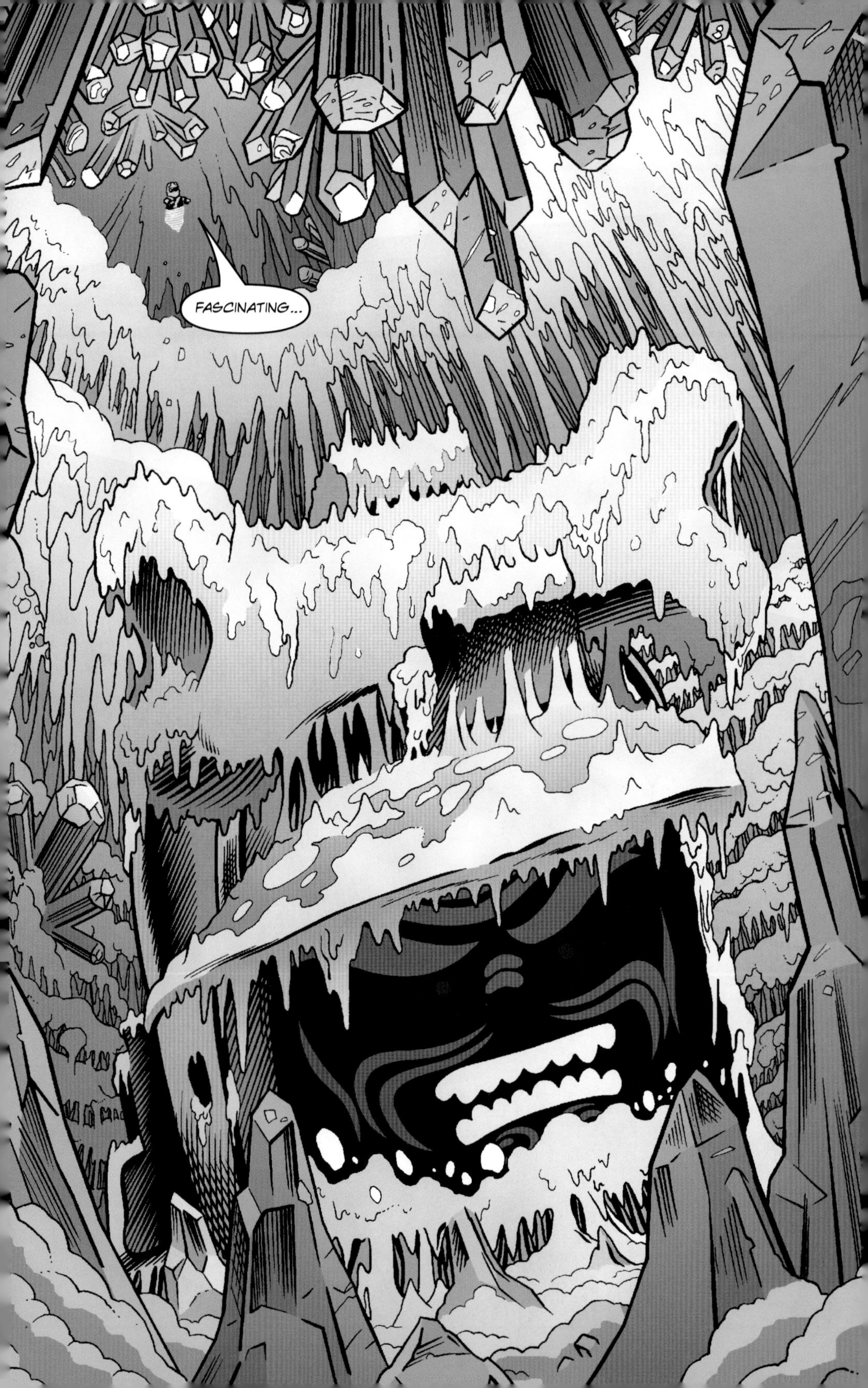
FASCINATING...

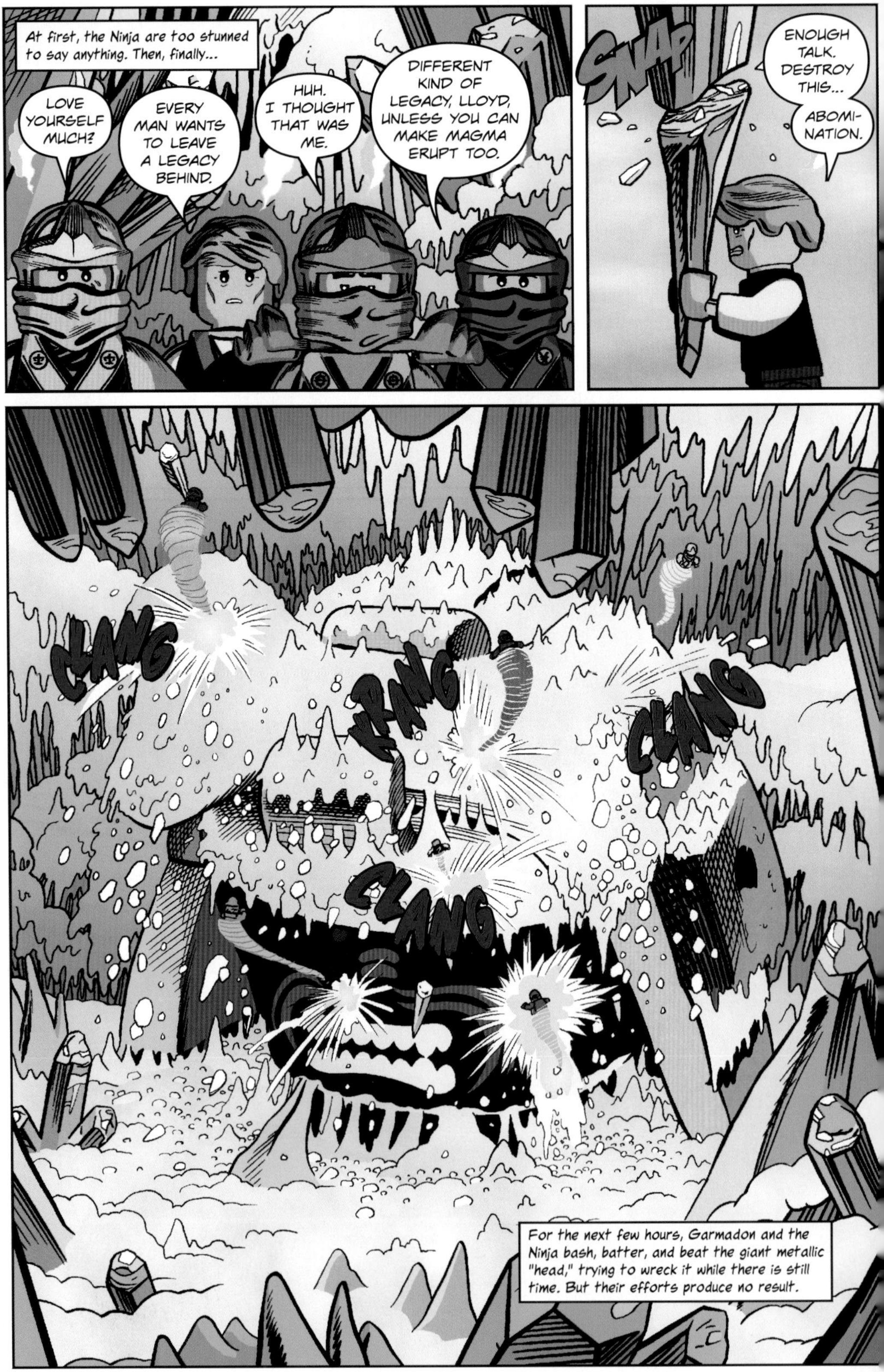
At first, the Ninja are too stunned to say anything. Then, finally...
LOVE YOURSELF MUCH?
EVERY MAN WANTS TO LEAVE A LEGACY BEHIND.
HUH. I THOUGHT THAT WAS ME.
DIFFERENT KIND OF LEGACY, LLOYD, UNLESS YOU CAN MAKE MAGMA ERUPT TOO.
SNAP
ENOUGH TALK. DESTROY THIS...
ABOMI-NATION.
CLANG
KRANG
CLANG
CLANG
For the next few hours, Garmadon and the Ninja bash, batter, and beat the giant metallic "head," trying to wreck it while there is still time. But their efforts produce no result.

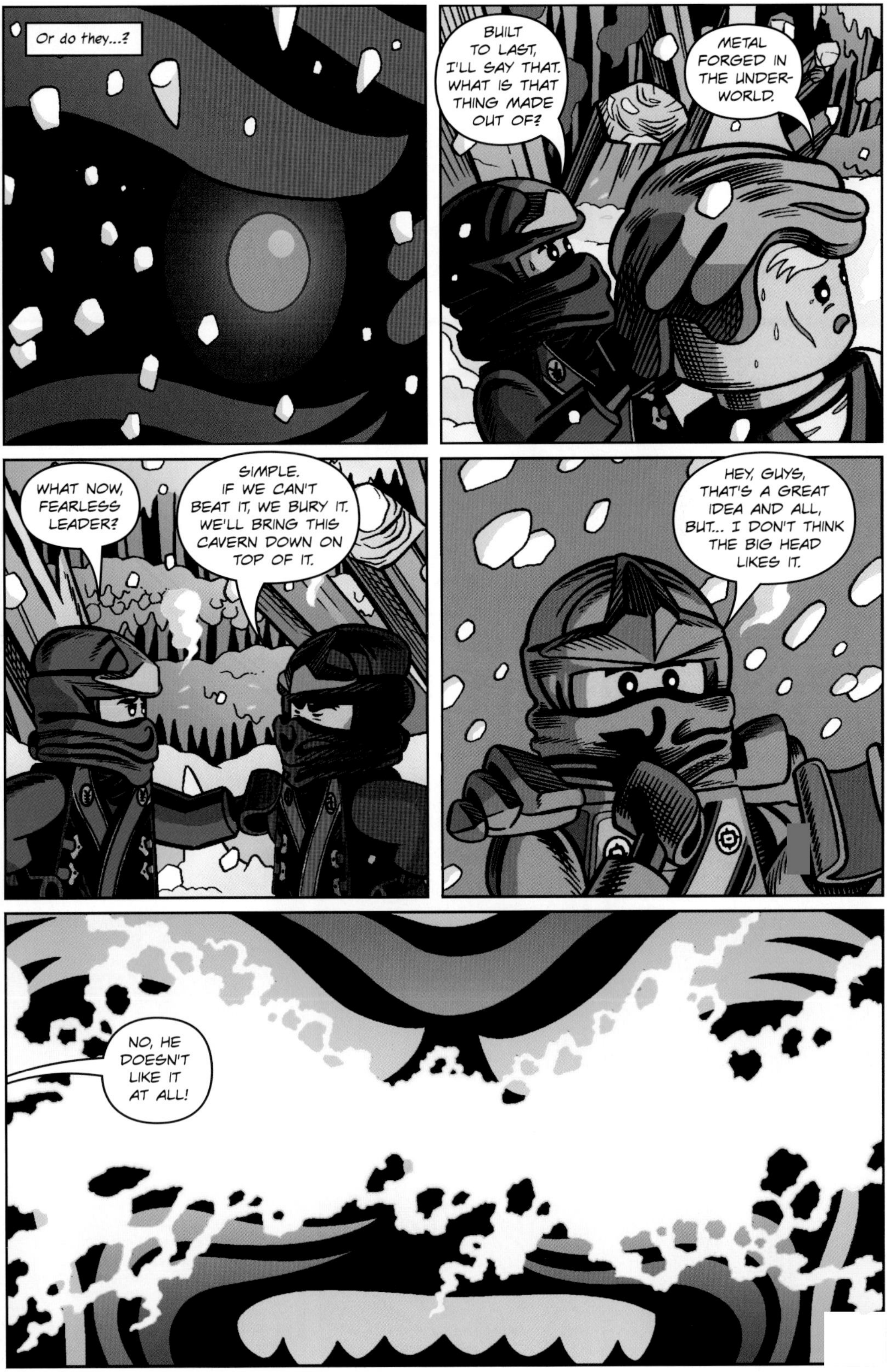
Or do they...?
BUILT TO LAST, I'LL SAY THAT. WHAT IS THAT THING MADE OUT OF?
METAL FORGED IN THE UNDER-WORLD.
WHAT NOW, FEARLESS LEADER?
SIMPLE. IF WE CAN'T BEAT IT, WE BURY IT. WE'LL BRING THIS CAVERN DOWN ON TOP OF IT.
HEY, GUYS, THAT'S A GREAT IDEA AND ALL, BUT... I DON'T THINK THE BIG HEAD LIKES IT.
NO, HE DOESN'T LIKE IT AT ALL!

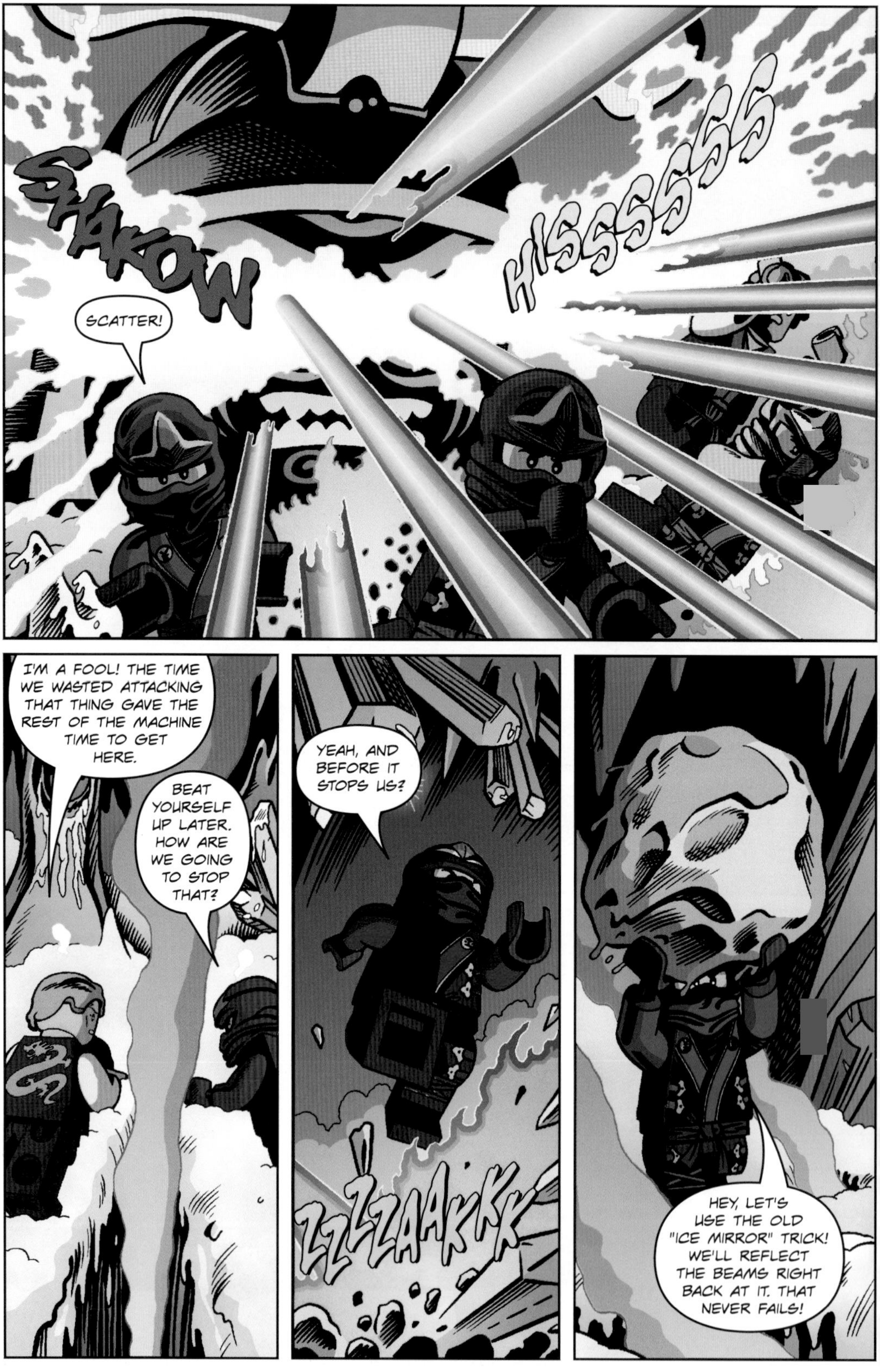

SHAKOW
HISSSSSSS
SCATTER!
I'M A FOOL! THE TIME WE WASTED ATTACKING THAT THING GAVE THE REST OF THE MACHINE TIME TO GET HERE.
BEAT YOURSELF UP LATER. HOW ARE WE GOING TO STOP THAT?
YEAH, AND BEFORE IT STOPS US?
ZZZZAAKKK
HEY, LET'S USE THE OLD "ICE MIRROR" TRICK! WE'LL REFLECT THE BEAMS RIGHT BACK AT IT. THAT NEVER FAILS!

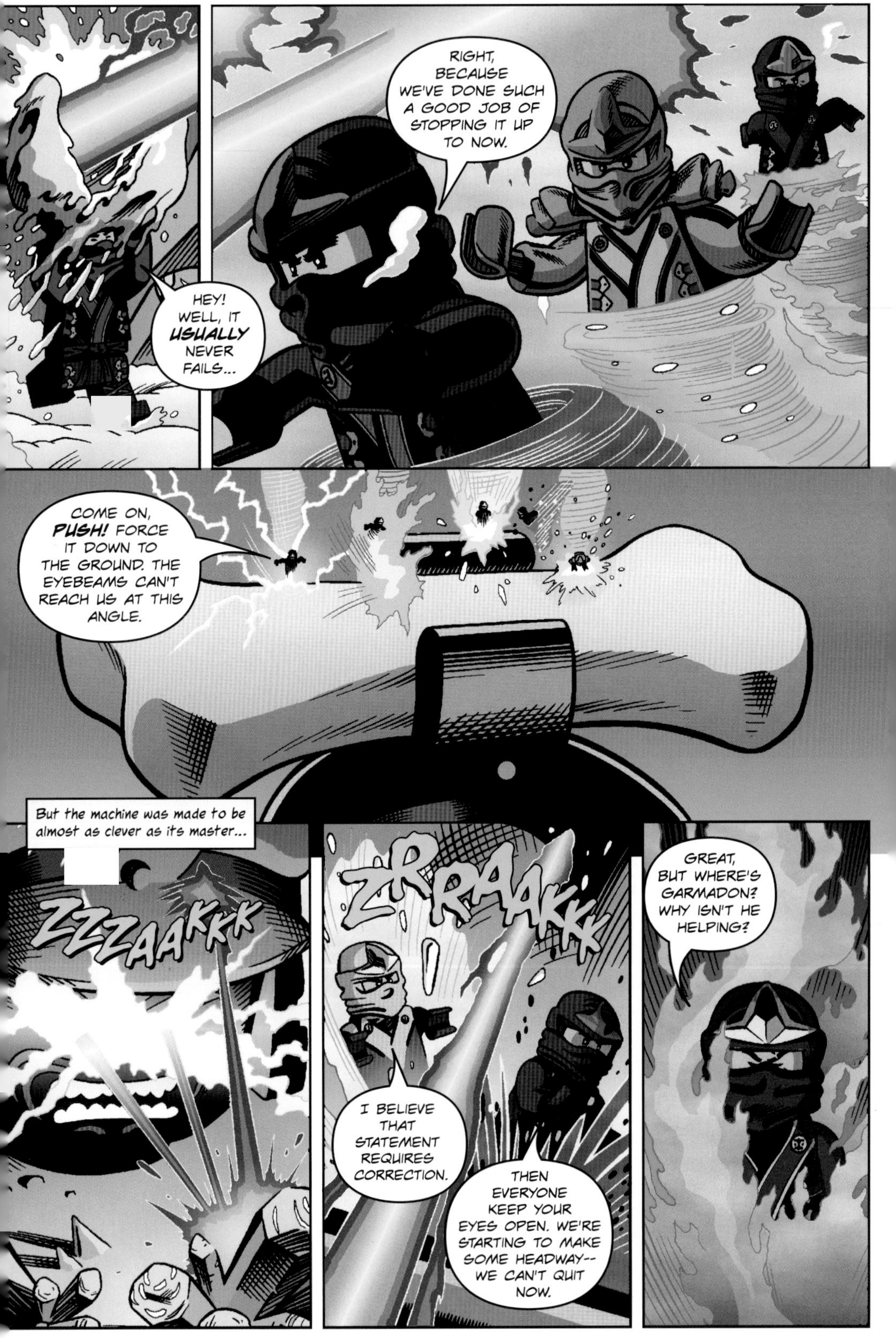
HEY! WELL, IT USUALLY NEVER FAILS...
RIGHT, BECAUSE WE'VE DONE SUCH A GOOD JOB OF STOPPING IT UP TO NOW.
COME ON, PUSH! FORCE IT DOWN TO THE GROUND. THE EYEBEAMS CAN'T REACH US AT THIS ANGLE.
But the machine was made to be almost as clever as its master...
ZZZAAKKK
ZRRAAKKK
I BELIEVE THAT STATEMENT REQUIRES CORRECTION.
THEN EVERYONE KEEP YOUR EYES OPEN. WE'RE STARTING TO MAKE SOME HEADWAY-- WE CAN'T QUIT NOW.
GREAT, BUT WHERE'S GARMADON? WHY ISN'T HE HELPING?

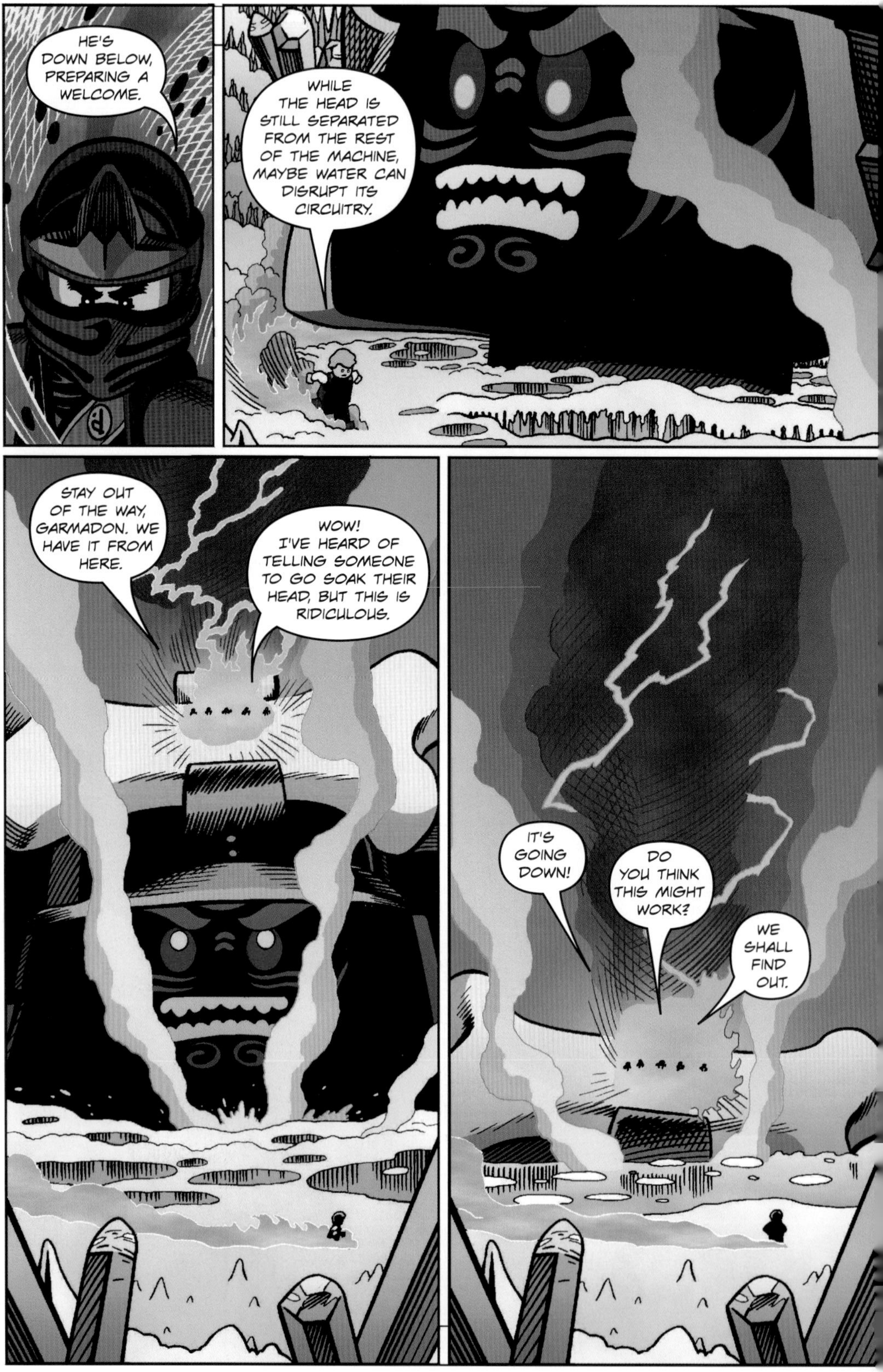
HE'S DOWN BELOW, PREPARING A WELCOME.
WHILE THE HEAD IS STILL SEPARATED FROM THE REST OF THE MACHINE, MAYBE WATER CAN DISRUPT ITS CIRCUITRY.
STAY OUT OF THE WAY, GARMADON. WE HAVE IT FROM HERE.
WOW! I'VE HEARD OF TELLING SOMEONE TO GO SOAK THEIR HEAD, BUT THIS IS RIDICULOUS.
IT'S GOING DOWN!
DO YOU THINK THIS MIGHT WORK?
WE SHALL FIND OUT.

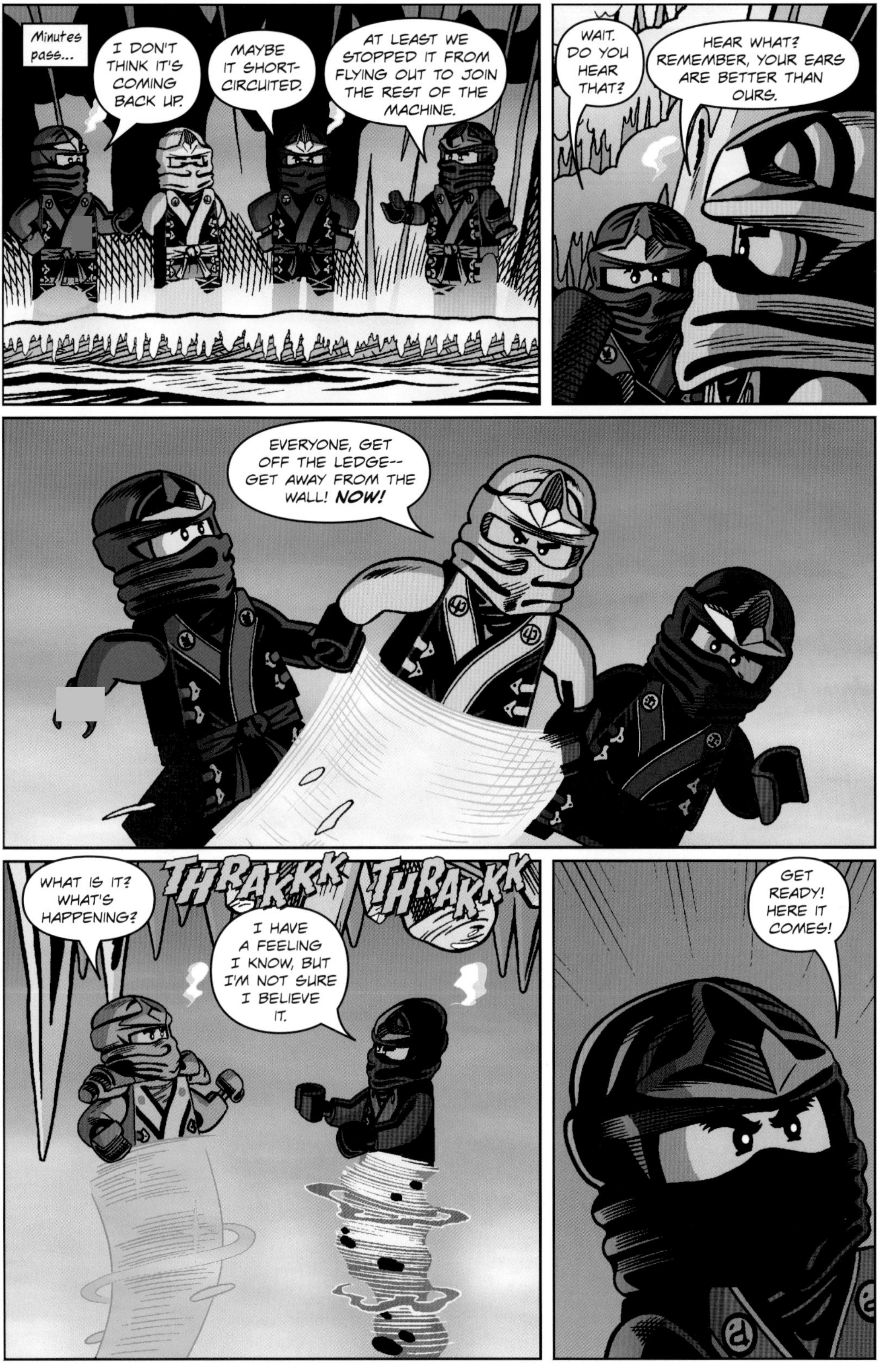
Minutes pass...
I DON'T THINK IT'S COMING BACK UP.
MAYBE IT SHORT-CIRCUITED.
AT LEAST WE STOPPED IT FROM FLYING OUT TO JOIN THE REST OF THE MACHINE.
WAIT. DO YOU HEAR THAT?
HEAR WHAT? REMEMBER, YOUR EARS ARE BETTER THAN OURS.
EVERYONE, GET OFF THE LEDGE-- GET AWAY FROM THE WALL! NOW!
THRAKKK THRAKKK
WHAT IS IT? WHAT'S HAPPENING?
I HAVE A FEELING I KNOW, BUT I'M NOT SURE I BELIEVE IT.
GET READY! HERE IT COMES!

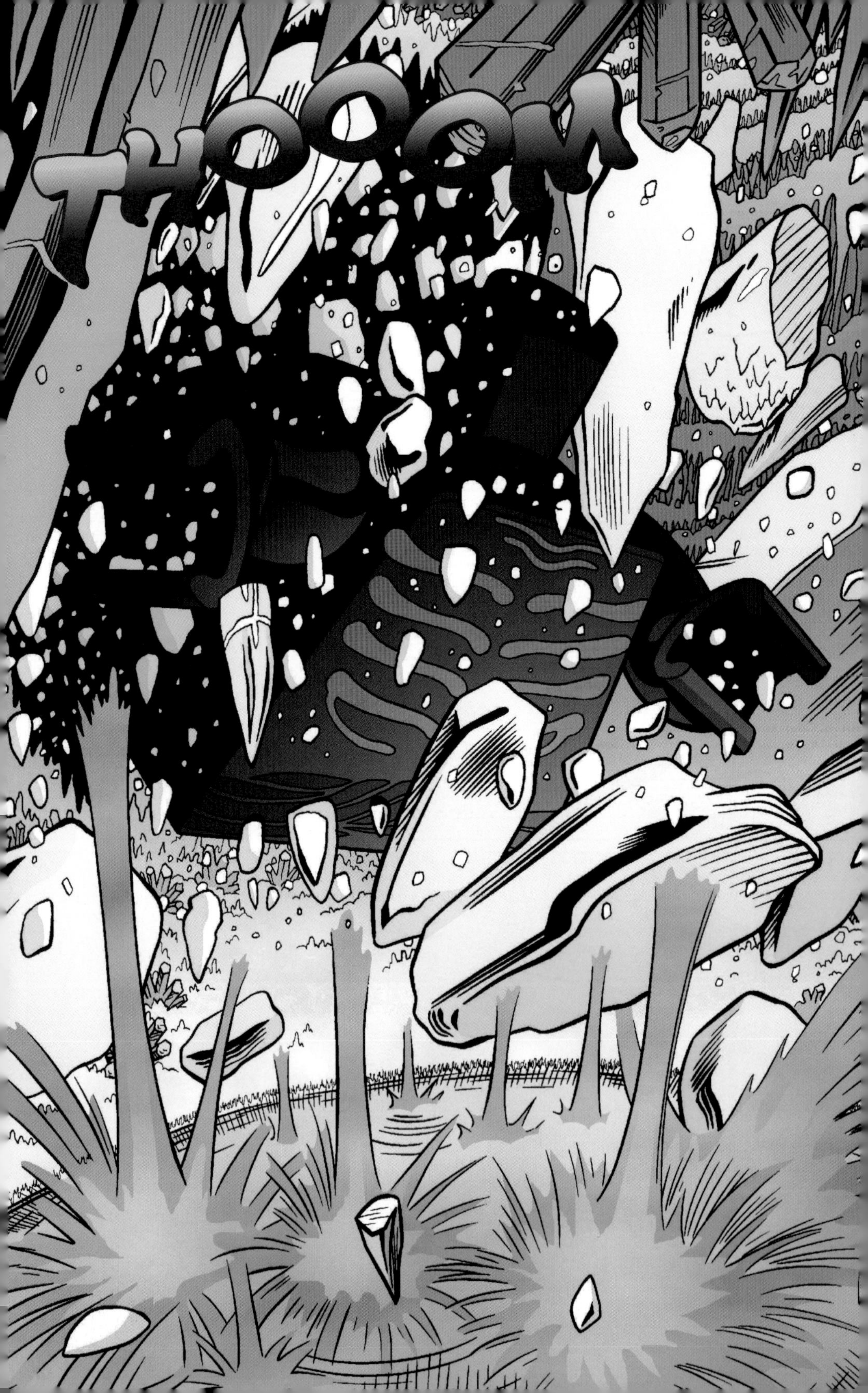
THOOOM

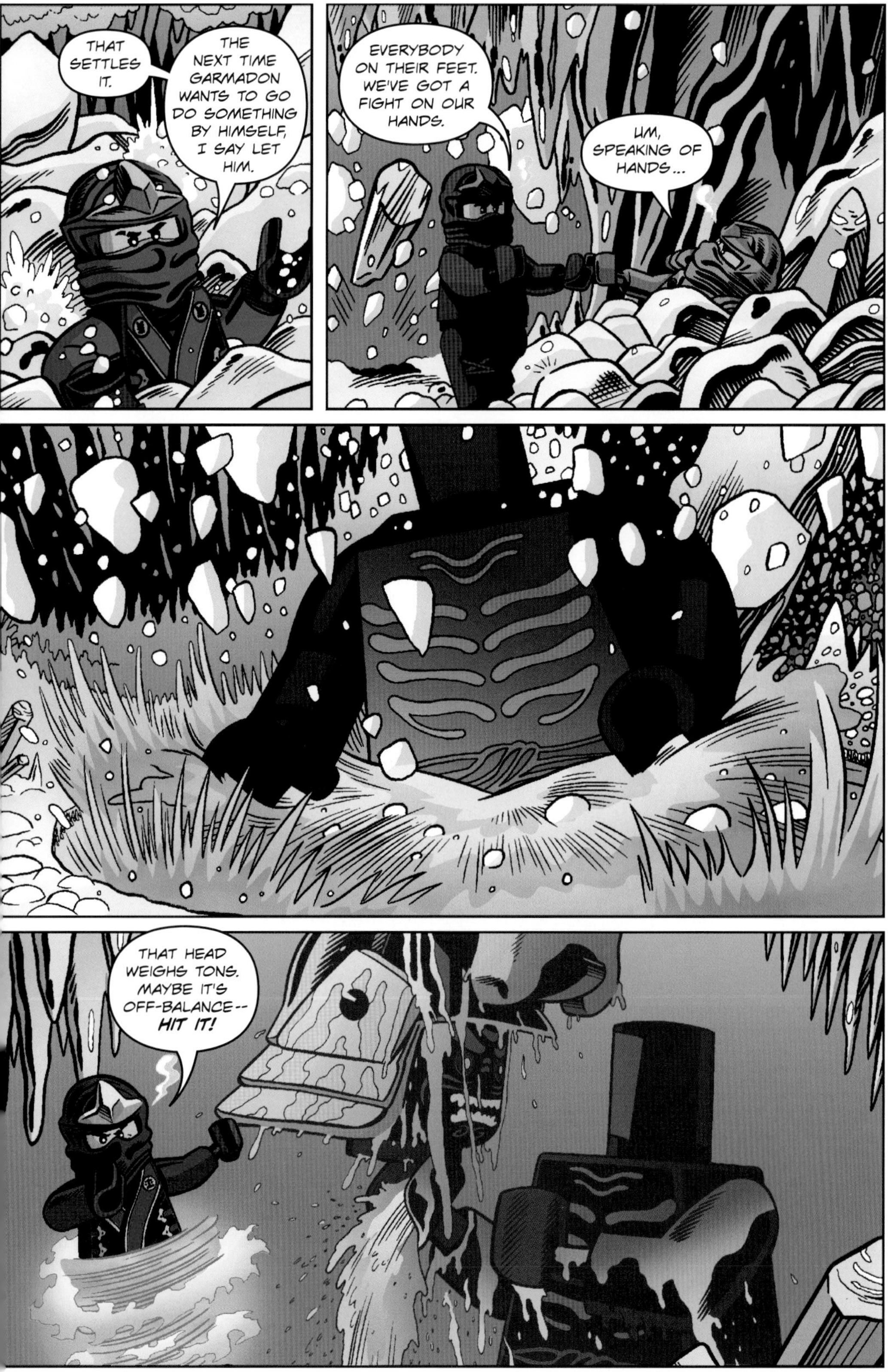
THAT SETTLES IT.
THE NEXT TIME GARMADON WANTS TO GO DO SOMETHING BY HIMSELF, I SAY LET HIM.
EVERYBODY ON THEIR FEET. WE'VE GOT A FIGHT ON OUR HANDS.
UM, SPEAKING OF HANDS...
THAT HEAD WEIGHS TONS. MAYBE IT'S OFF-BALANCE-- ***HIT IT!***

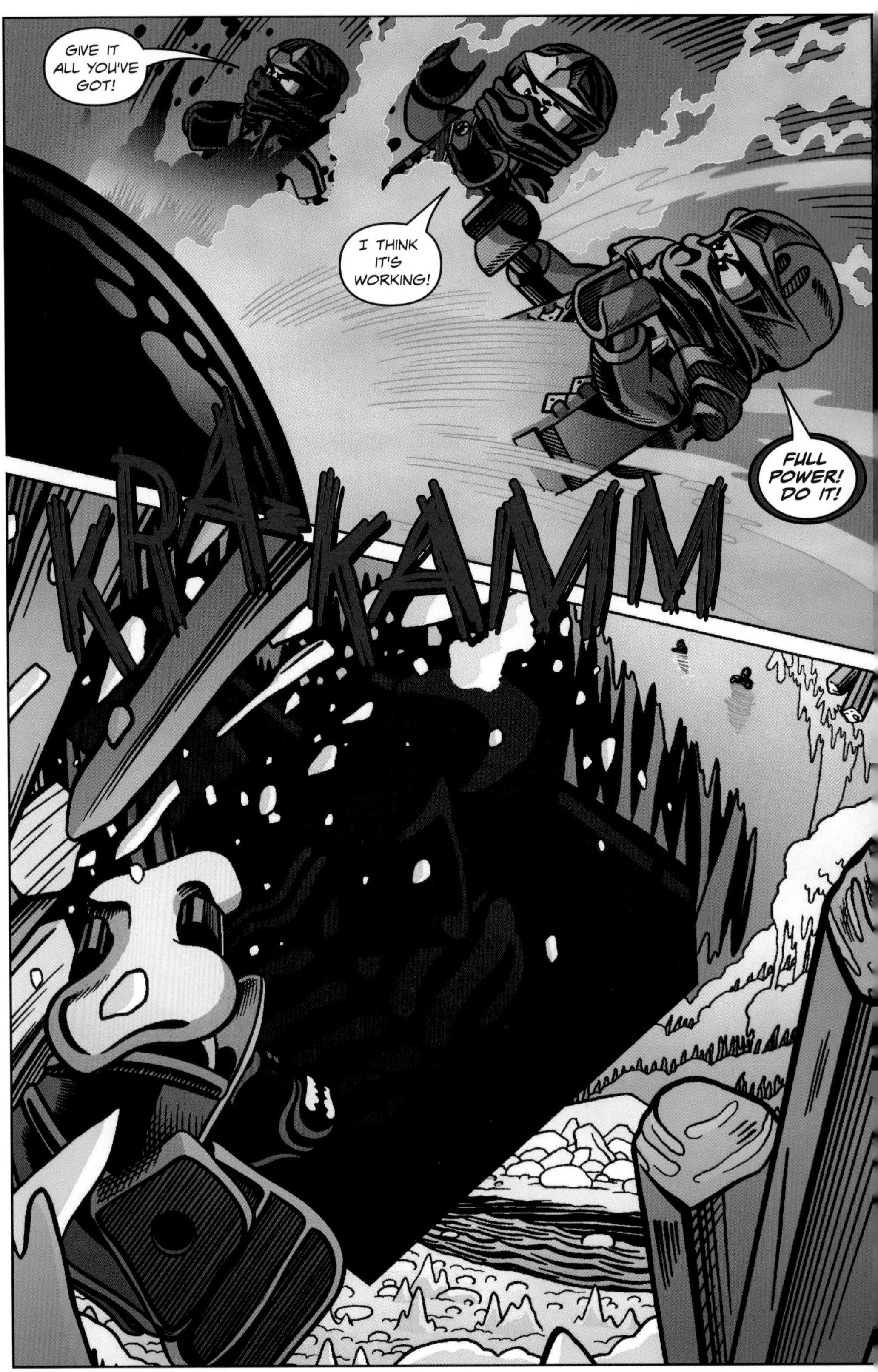
GIVE IT ALL YOU'VE GOT!
I THINK IT'S WORKING!
FULL POWER! DO IT!
KRA-KAMM

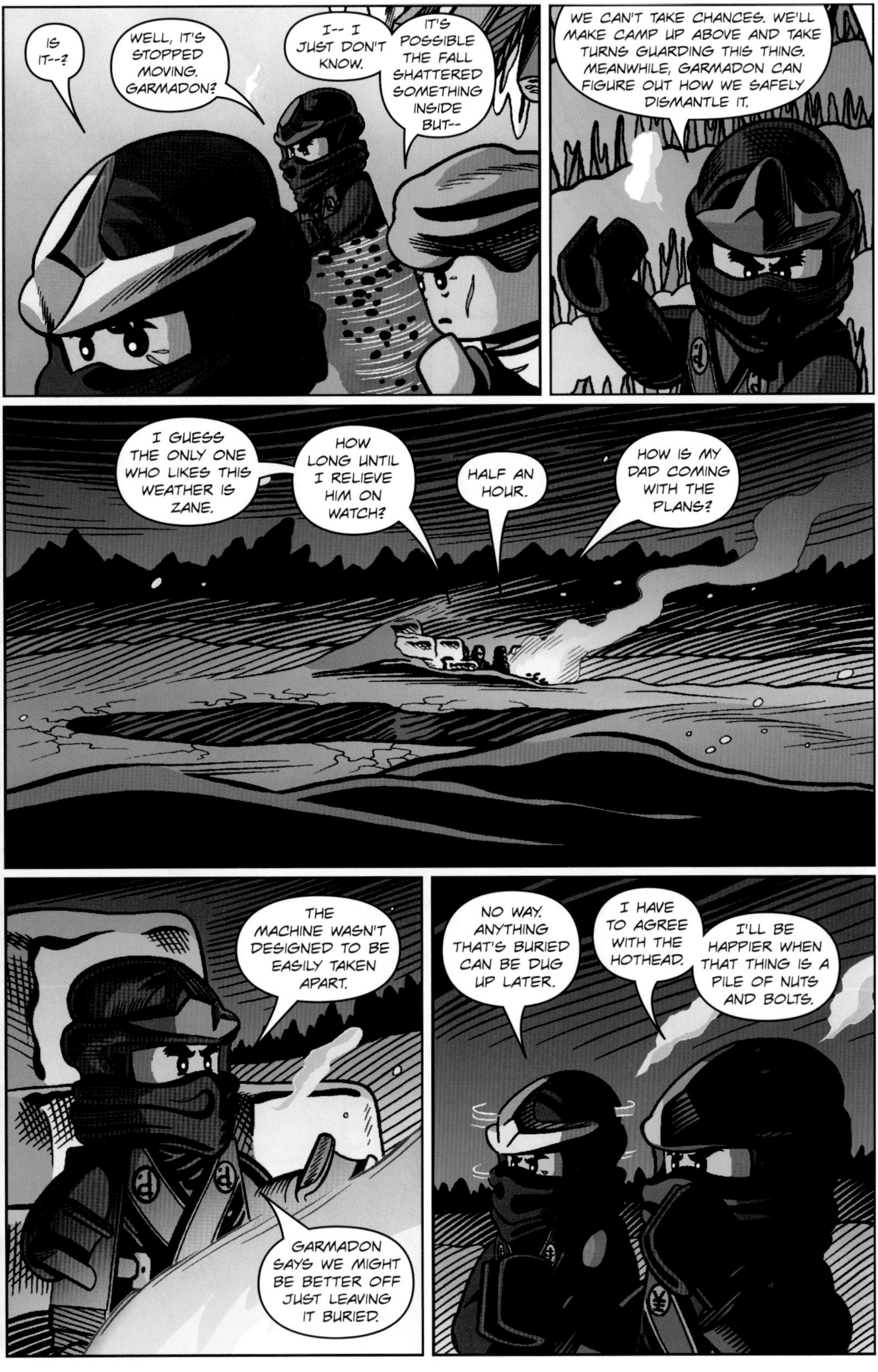
IS IT--?
WELL, IT'S STOPPED MOVING. GARMADON?
I-- I JUST DON'T KNOW.
IT'S POSSIBLE THE FALL SHATTERED SOMETHING INSIDE BUT--
WE CAN'T TAKE CHANCES. WE'LL MAKE CAMP UP ABOVE AND TAKE TURNS GUARDING THIS THING. MEANWHILE, GARMADON CAN FIGURE OUT HOW WE SAFELY DISMANTLE IT.
I GUESS THE ONLY ONE WHO LIKES THIS WEATHER IS ZANE.
HOW LONG UNTIL I RELIEVE HIM ON WATCH?
HALF AN HOUR.
HOW IS MY DAD COMING WITH THE PLANS?
THE MACHINE WASN'T DESIGNED TO BE EASILY TAKEN APART.
GARMADON SAYS WE MIGHT BE BETTER OFF JUST LEAVING IT BURIED.
NO WAY. ANYTHING THAT'S BURIED CAN BE DUG UP LATER.
I HAVE TO AGREE WITH THE HOTHEAD.
I'LL BE HAPPIER WHEN THAT THING IS A PILE OF NUTS AND BOLTS.

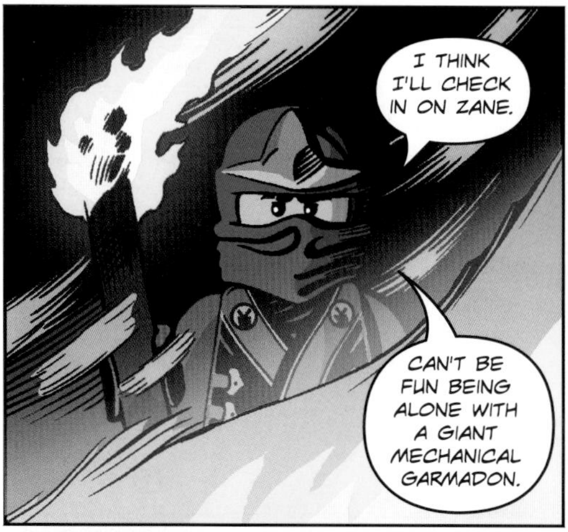
I THINK I'LL CHECK IN ON ZANE.
CAN'T BE FUN BEING ALONE WITH A GIANT MECHANICAL GARMADON.

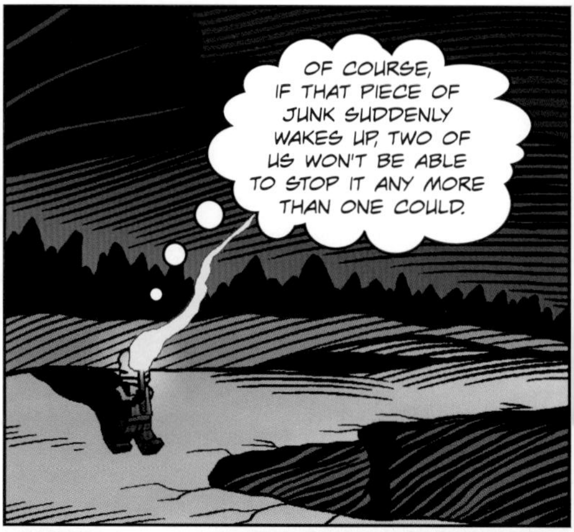
OF COURSE, IF THAT PIECE OF JUNK SUDDENLY WAKES UP, TWO OF US WON'T BE ABLE TO STOP IT ANY MORE THAN ONE COULD.

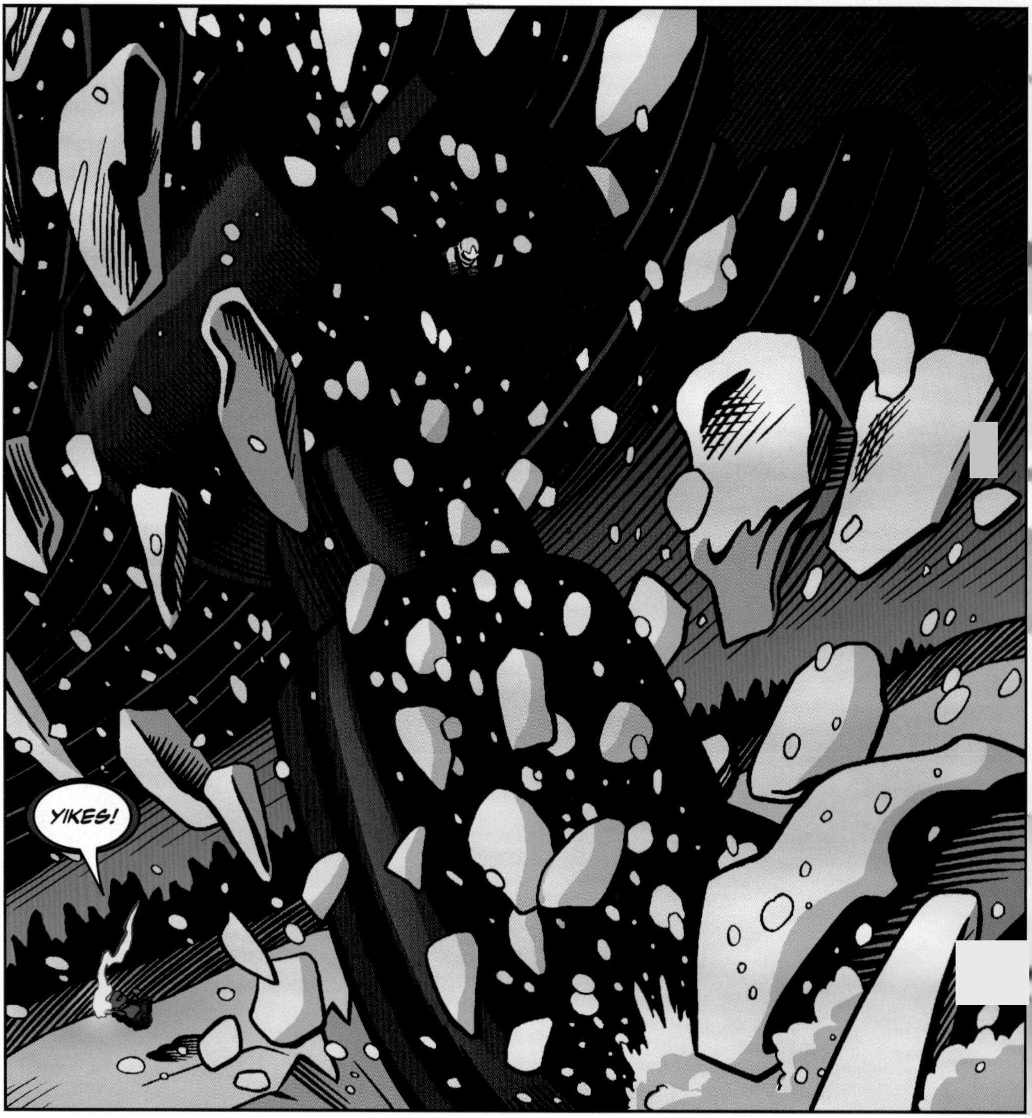
YIKES!

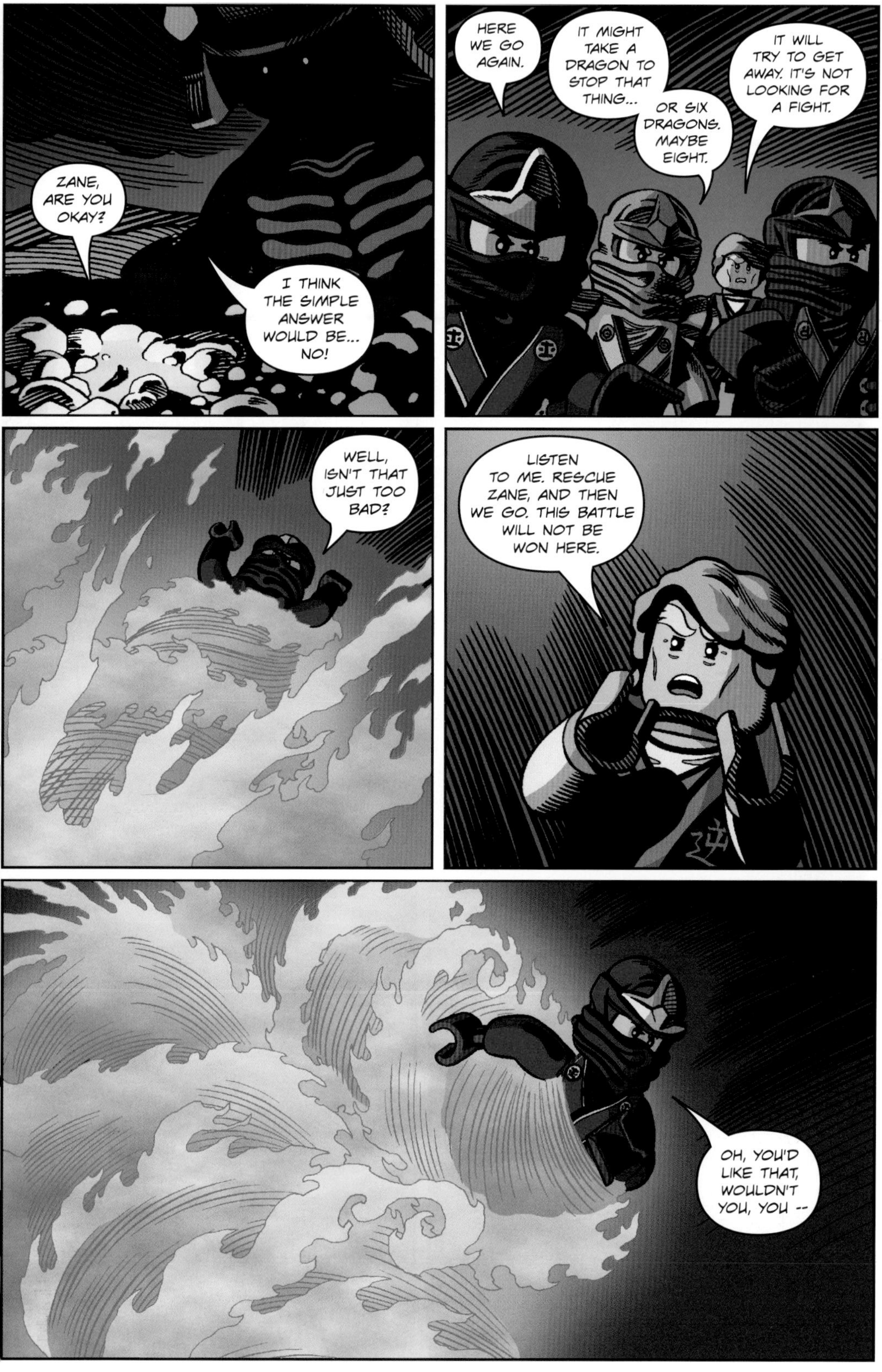
ZANE, ARE YOU OKAY?
I THINK THE SIMPLE ANSWER WOULD BE... NO!
HERE WE GO AGAIN.
IT MIGHT TAKE A DRAGON TO STOP THAT THING...
OR SIX DRAGONS. MAYBE EIGHT.
IT WILL TRY TO GET AWAY. IT'S NOT LOOKING FOR A FIGHT.
WELL, ISN'T THAT JUST TOO BAD?
LISTEN TO ME. RESCUE ZANE, AND THEN WE GO. THIS BATTLE WILL NOT BE WON HERE.
OH, YOU'D LIKE THAT, WOULDN'T YOU, YOU --

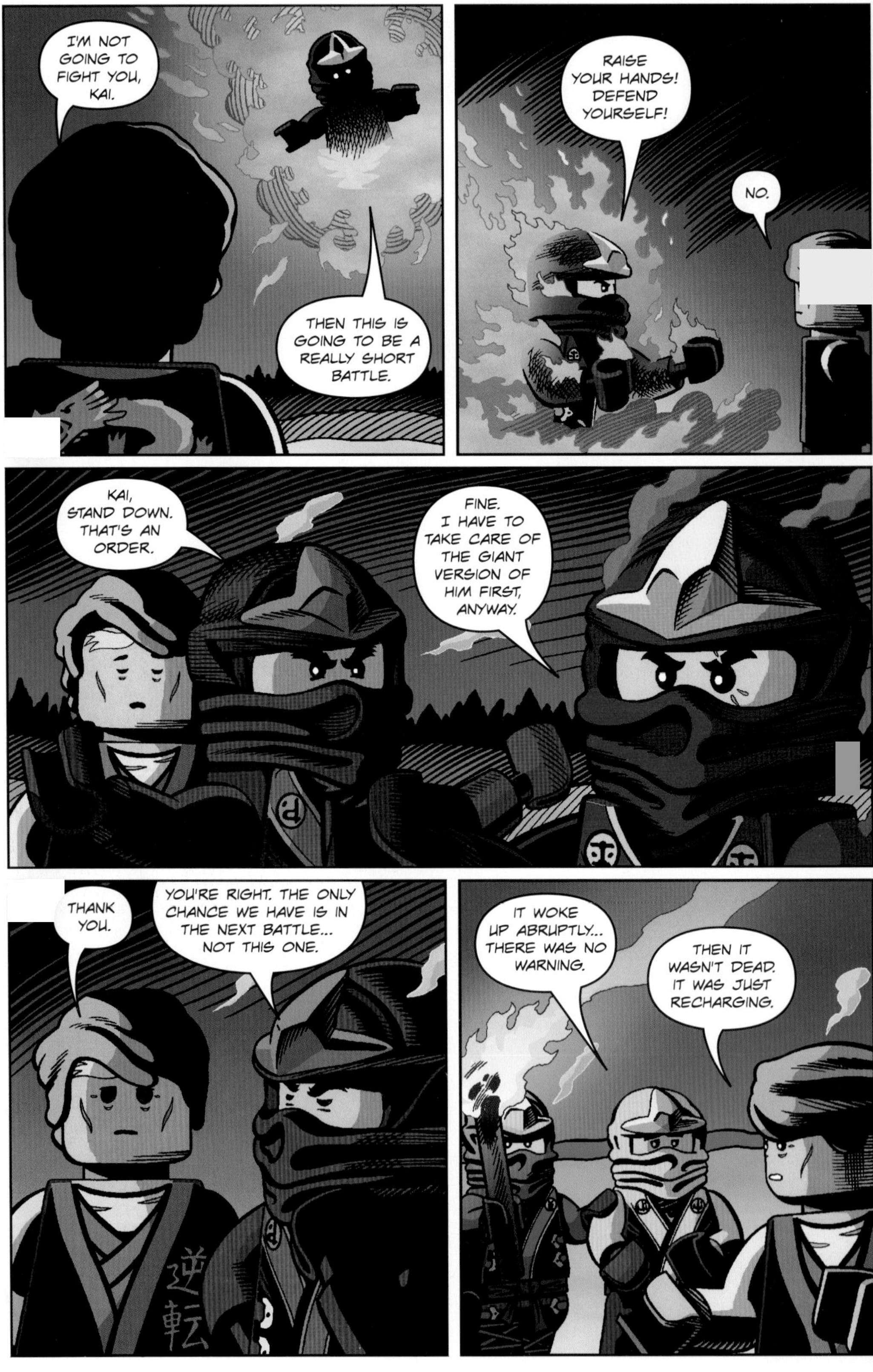
I'M NOT GOING TO FIGHT YOU, KAI.
THEN THIS IS GOING TO BE A REALLY SHORT BATTLE.
RAISE YOUR HANDS! DEFEND YOURSELF!
NO.
KAI, STAND DOWN. THAT'S AN ORDER.
FINE. I HAVE TO TAKE CARE OF THE GIANT VERSION OF HIM FIRST, ANYWAY.
THANK YOU.
YOU'RE RIGHT. THE ONLY CHANCE WE HAVE IS IN THE NEXT BATTLE... NOT THIS ONE.
IT WOKE UP ABRUPTLY... THERE WAS NO WARNING.
THEN IT WASN'T DEAD. IT WAS JUST RECHARGING.

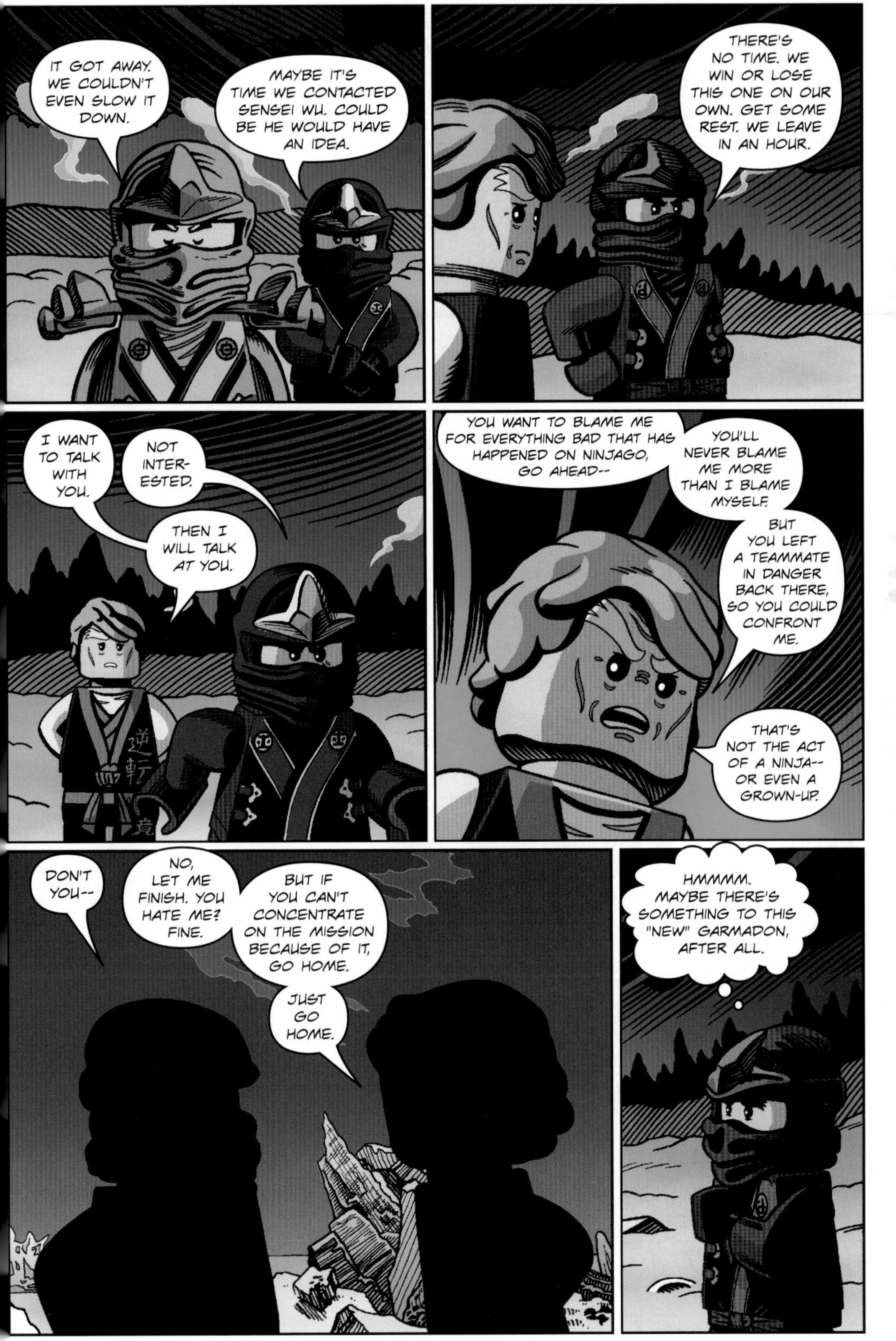
IT GOT AWAY. WE COULDN'T EVEN SLOW IT DOWN.
MAYBE IT'S TIME WE CONTACTED SENSEI WU. COULD BE HE WOULD HAVE AN IDEA.
THERE'S NO TIME. WE WIN OR LOSE THIS ONE ON OUR OWN. GET SOME REST. WE LEAVE IN AN HOUR.
I WANT TO TALK WITH YOU.
NOT INTER-ESTED.
THEN I WILL TALK AT YOU.
YOU WANT TO BLAME ME FOR EVERYTHING BAD THAT HAS HAPPENED ON NINJAGO, GO AHEAD--
YOU'LL NEVER BLAME ME MORE THAN I BLAME MYSELF.
BUT YOU LEFT A TEAMMATE IN DANGER BACK THERE, SO YOU COULD CONFRONT ME.
THAT'S NOT THE ACT OF A NINJA-- OR EVEN A GROWN-UP.
DON'T YOU--
NO, LET ME FINISH. YOU HATE ME? FINE.
BUT IF YOU CAN'T CONCENTRATE ON THE MISSION BECAUSE OF IT, GO HOME.
JUST GO HOME.
HMMMM. MAYBE THERE'S SOMETHING TO THIS "NEW" GARMADON, AFTER ALL.

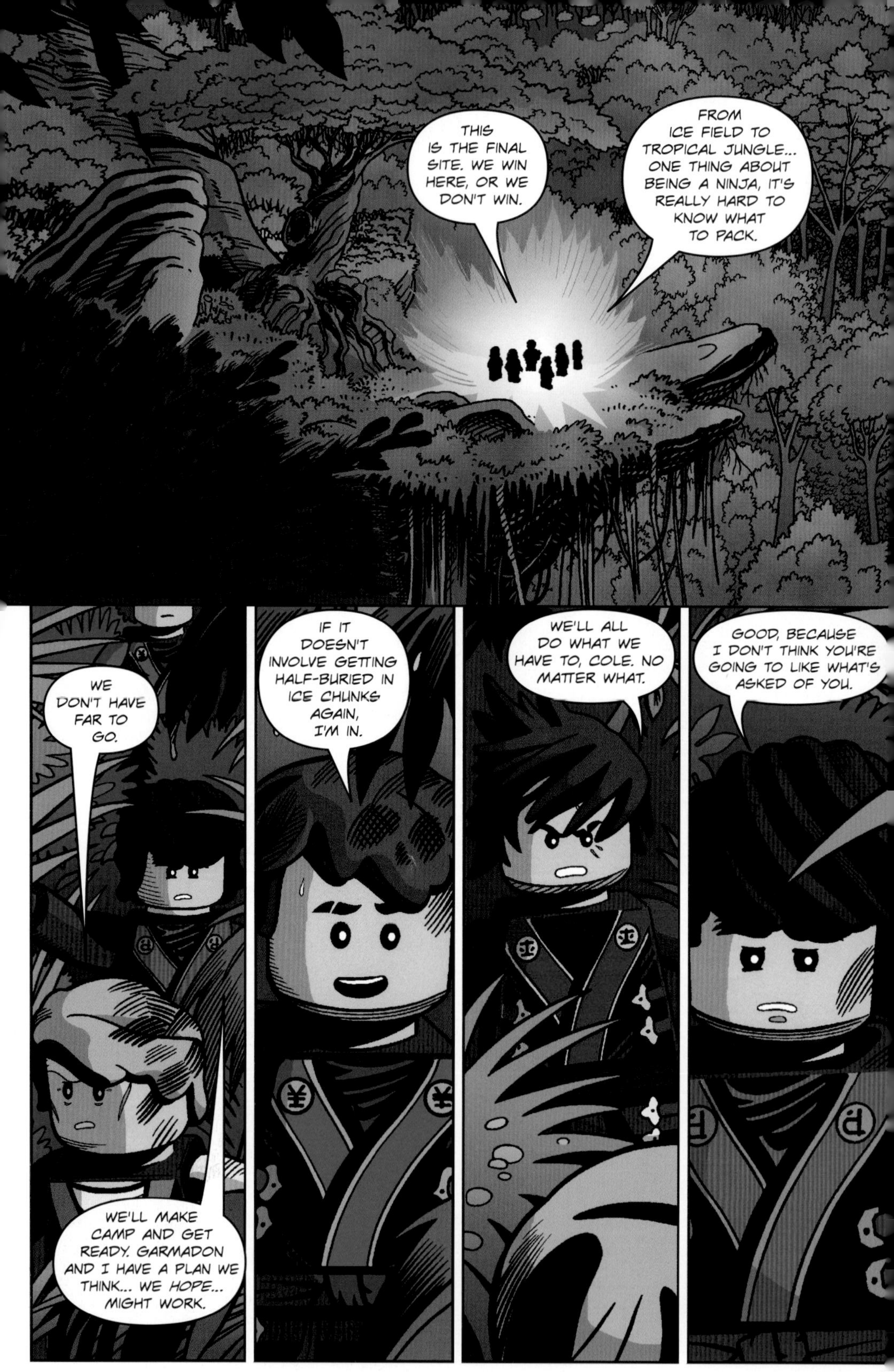
THIS IS THE FINAL SITE. WE WIN HERE, OR WE DON'T WIN.
FROM ICE FIELD TO TROPICAL JUNGLE... ONE THING ABOUT BEING A NINJA, IT'S REALLY HARD TO KNOW WHAT TO PACK.
WE DON'T HAVE FAR TO GO.
WE'LL MAKE CAMP AND GET READY. GARMADON AND I HAVE A PLAN WE THINK... WE HOPE... MIGHT WORK.
IF IT DOESN'T INVOLVE GETTING HALF-BURIED IN ICE CHUNKS AGAIN, I'M IN.
WE'LL ALL DO WHAT WE HAVE TO, COLE. NO MATTER WHAT.
GOOD, BECAUSE I DON'T THINK YOU'RE GOING TO LIKE WHAT'S ASKED OF YOU.

That night...

SO WE'RE AGREED?

YES. OUR LAST, BEST OPPORTUNITY MAY BE WHEN THE MACHINE IS WHOLE, STRANGE AS THAT MIGHT SOUND.

PROBABLY. EVERY PART THAT YOU DESIGNED SEEMS TO BE INVULNERABLE. SAMUKAI DESIGNED THE LAST PART. I'M HOPING HE'S NOT THE ENGINEER YOU ARE.

NOW I HAVE A QUESTION FOR YOU... WHY DID YOU LET US COME ALONG? YOU COULD HAVE WALKED THROUGH ONE OF YOUR GATES AND DISAPPEARED WHENEVER YOU LIKED.

MAYBE I FELT I NEEDED TO PROVE SOMETHING TO LLOYD, TO THE REST OF YOU... AND TO MYSELF.

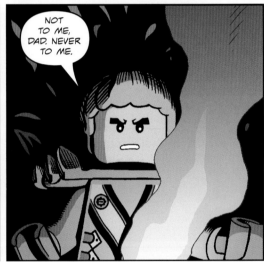

NOT TO ME, DAD. NEVER TO ME.

COLE, IF YOU DON'T MIND, I'D LIKE TO TALK TO MY DAD.

I'M GOING TO GET SOME SLEEP. I THINK TOMORROW IS GOING TO BE A LONG DAY FOR US ALL.

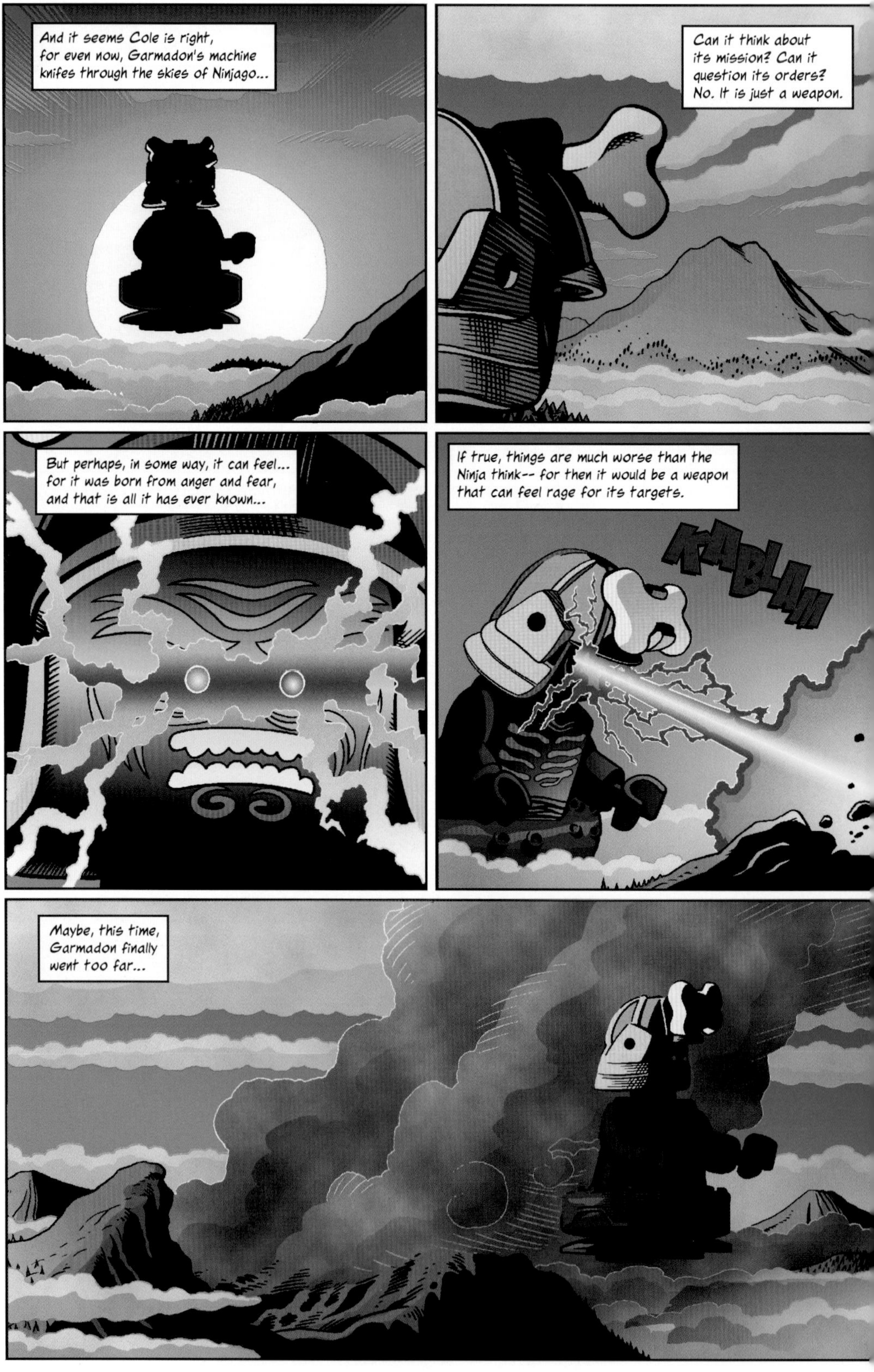
And it seems Cole is right, for even now, Garmadon's machine knifes through the skies of Ninjago...
Can it think about its mission? Can it question its orders? No. It is just a weapon.
But perhaps, in some way, it can feel... for it was born from anger and fear, and that is all it has ever known...
If true, things are much worse than the Ninja think-- for then it would be a weapon that can feel rage for its targets.
KABLAM
Maybe, this time, Garmadon finally went too far...

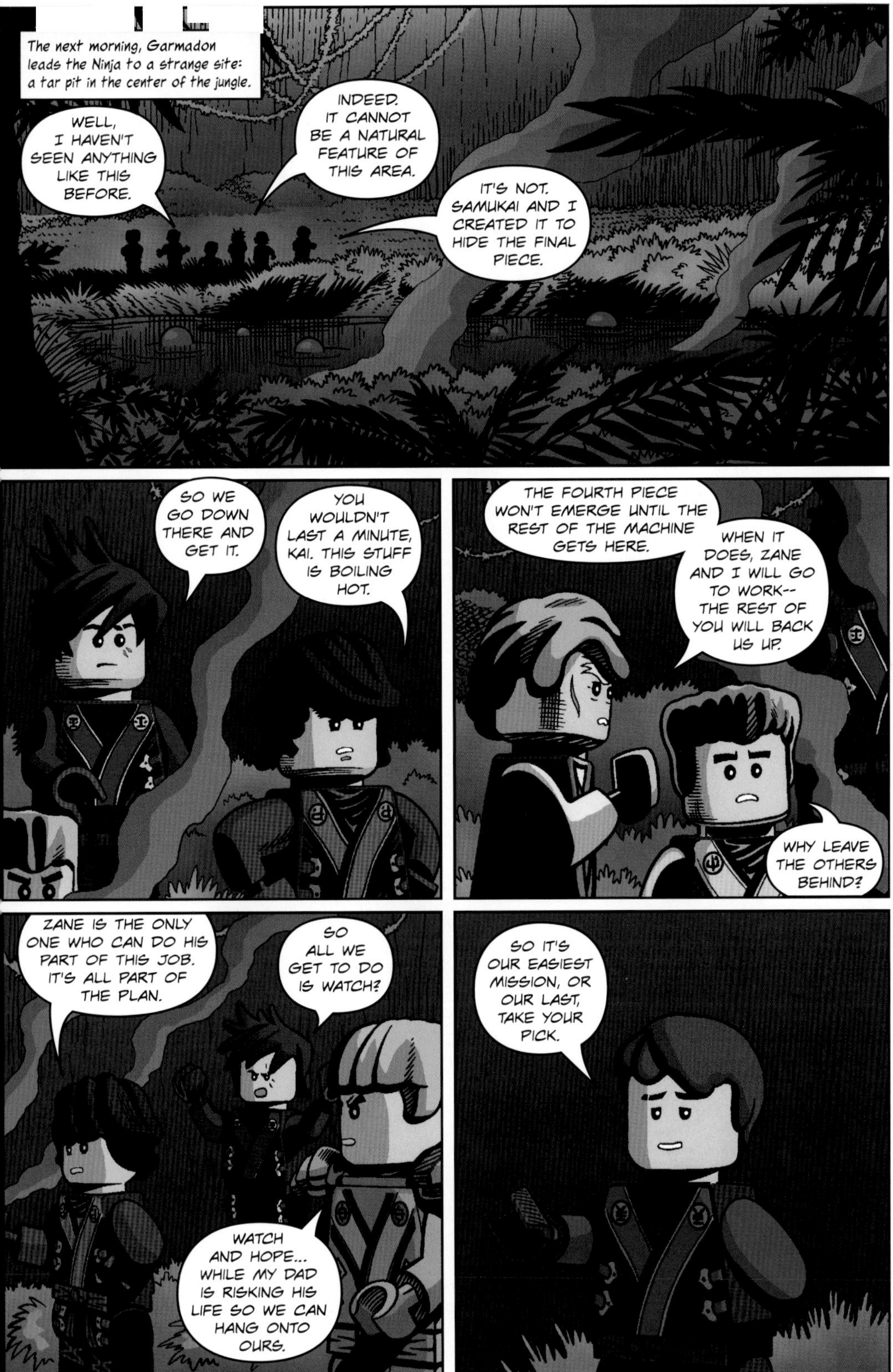

The next morning, Garmadon leads the Ninja to a strange site: a tar pit in the center of the jungle.
WELL, I HAVEN'T SEEN ANYTHING LIKE THIS BEFORE.
INDEED. IT CANNOT BE A NATURAL FEATURE OF THIS AREA.
IT'S NOT. SAMUKAI AND I CREATED IT TO HIDE THE FINAL PIECE.
SO WE GO DOWN THERE AND GET IT.
YOU WOULDN'T LAST A MINUTE, KAI. THIS STUFF IS BOILING HOT.
THE FOURTH PIECE WON'T EMERGE UNTIL THE REST OF THE MACHINE GETS HERE.
WHEN IT DOES, ZANE AND I WILL GO TO WORK-- THE REST OF YOU WILL BACK US UP.
WHY LEAVE THE OTHERS BEHIND?
ZANE IS THE ONLY ONE WHO CAN DO HIS PART OF THIS JOB. IT'S ALL PART OF THE PLAN.
SO ALL WE GET TO DO IS WATCH?
WATCH AND HOPE... WHILE MY DAD IS RISKING HIS LIFE SO WE CAN HANG ONTO OURS.
SO IT'S OUR EASIEST MISSION, OR OUR LAST, TAKE YOUR PICK.

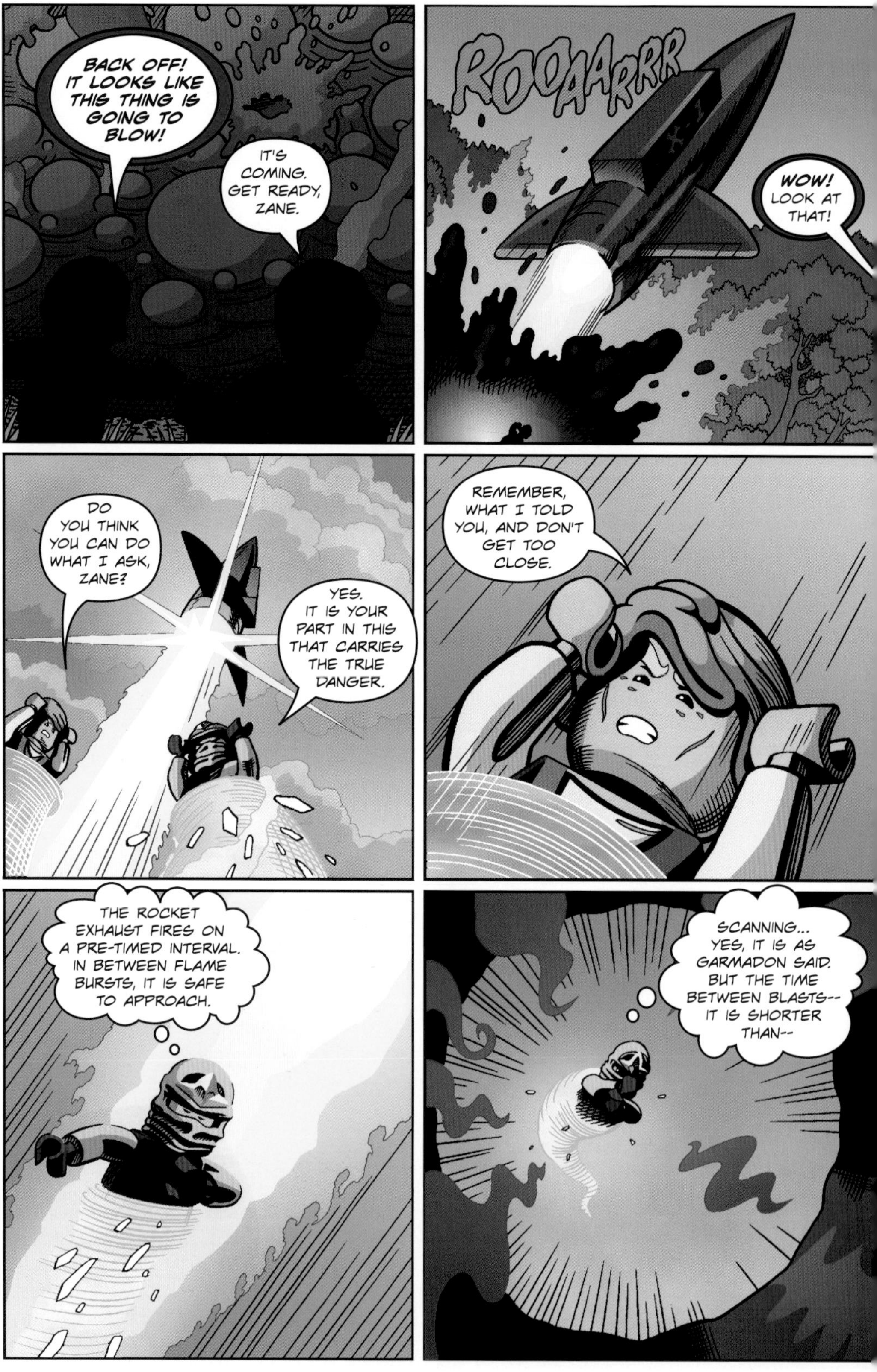
BACK OFF! IT LOOKS LIKE THIS THING IS GOING TO BLOW!
IT'S COMING. GET READY, ZANE.
ROOOAARRR
WOW! LOOK AT THAT!
DO YOU THINK YOU CAN DO WHAT I ASK, ZANE?
YES. IT IS YOUR PART IN THIS THAT CARRIES THE TRUE DANGER.
REMEMBER, WHAT I TOLD YOU, AND DON'T GET TOO CLOSE.
THE ROCKET EXHAUST FIRES ON A PRE-TIMED INTERVAL. IN BETWEEN FLAME BURSTS, IT IS SAFE TO APPROACH.
SCANNING... YES, IT IS AS GARMADON SAID. BUT THE TIME BETWEEN BLASTS-- IT IS SHORTER THAN--

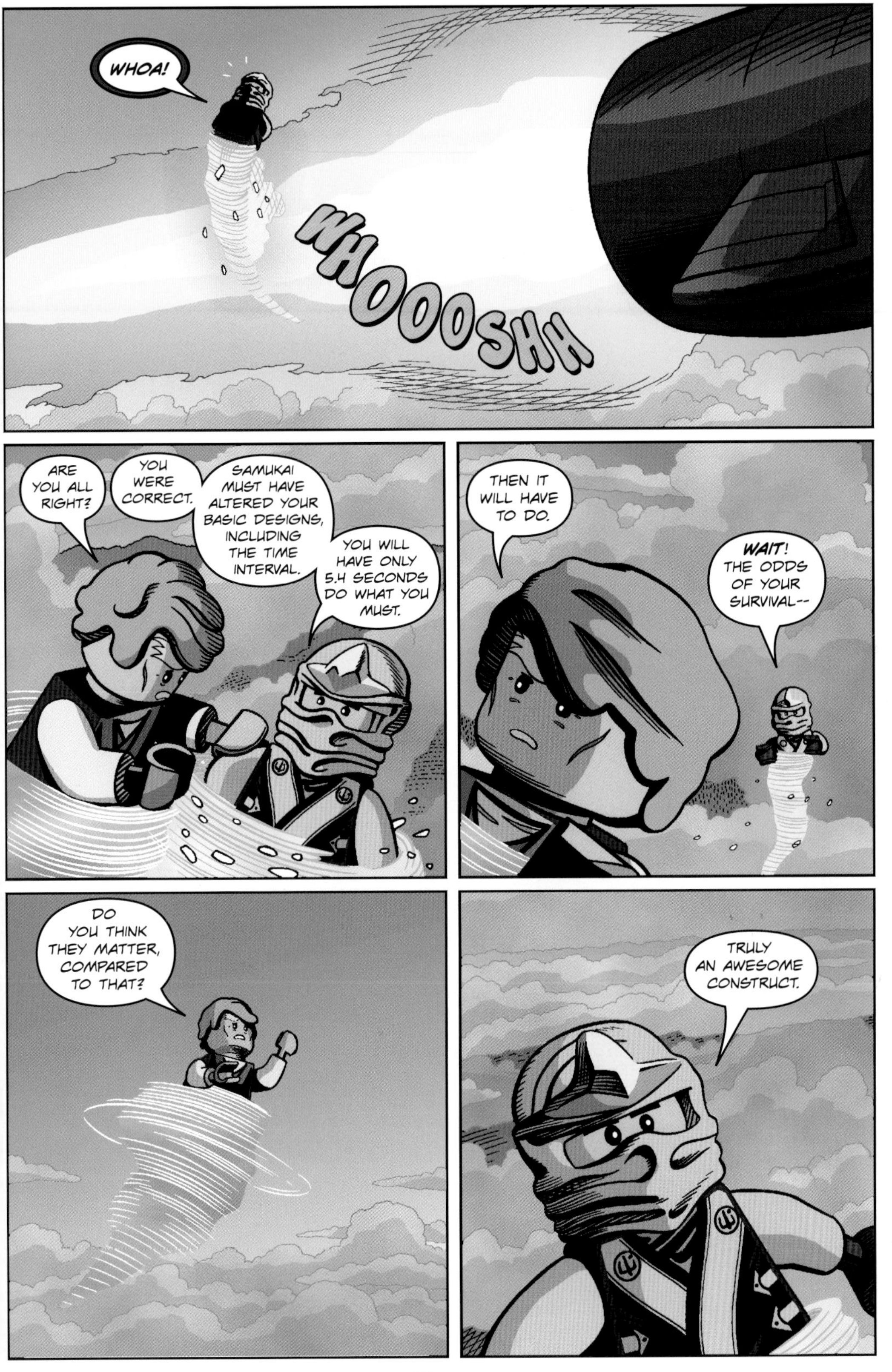
WHOA!
WHOOOOSHH
ARE YOU ALL RIGHT?
YOU WERE CORRECT.
SAMUKAI MUST HAVE ALTERED YOUR BASIC DESIGNS, INCLUDING THE TIME INTERVAL.
YOU WILL HAVE ONLY 5.4 SECONDS DO WHAT YOU MUST.
THEN IT WILL HAVE TO DO.
WAIT! THE ODDS OF YOUR SURVIVAL--
DO YOU THINK THEY MATTER, COMPARED TO THAT?
TRULY AN AWESOME CONSTRUCT.

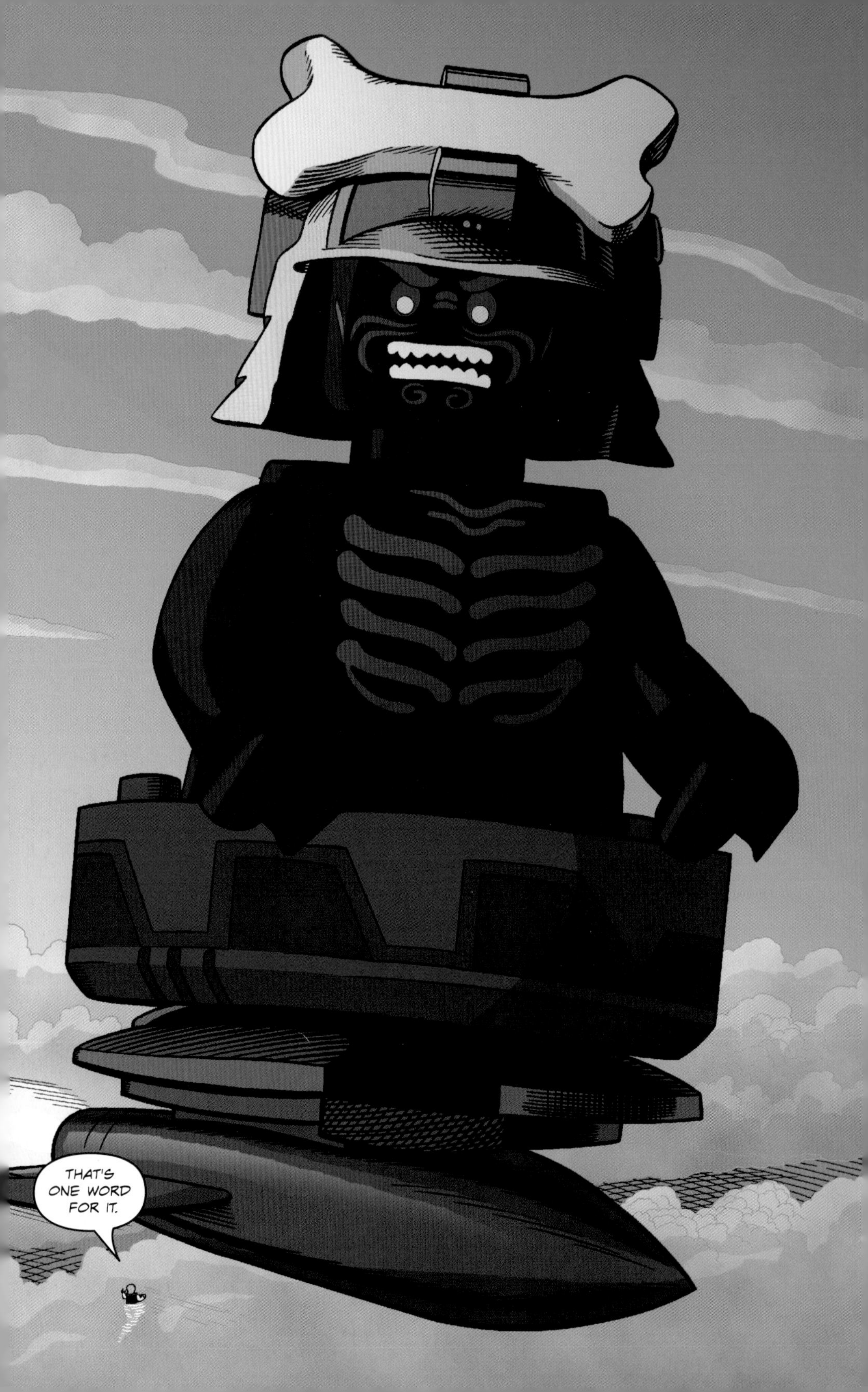
THAT'S ONE WORD FOR IT.

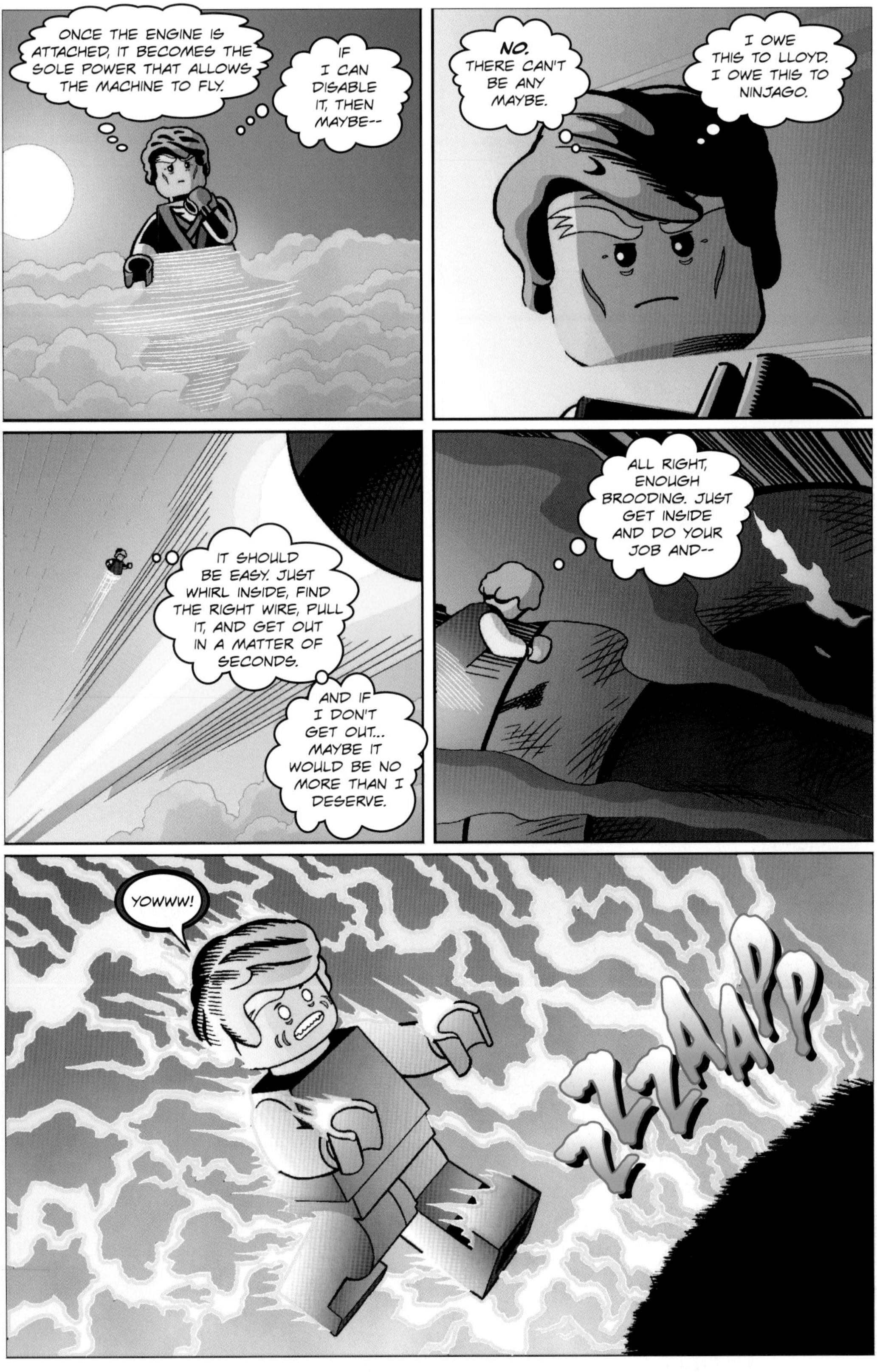
ONCE THE ENGINE IS ATTACHED, IT BECOMES THE SOLE POWER THAT ALLOWS THE MACHINE TO FLY.
IF I CAN DISABLE IT, THEN MAYBE--
NO. THERE CAN'T BE ANY MAYBE.
I OWE THIS TO LLOYD. I OWE THIS TO NINJAGO.
IT SHOULD BE EASY. JUST WHIRL INSIDE, FIND THE RIGHT WIRE, PULL IT, AND GET OUT IN A MATTER OF SECONDS.
AND IF I DON'T GET OUT... MAYBE IT WOULD BE NO MORE THAN I DESERVE.
ALL RIGHT, ENOUGH BROODING. JUST GET INSIDE AND DO YOUR JOB AND--
YOWWW!
ZZZAAPP

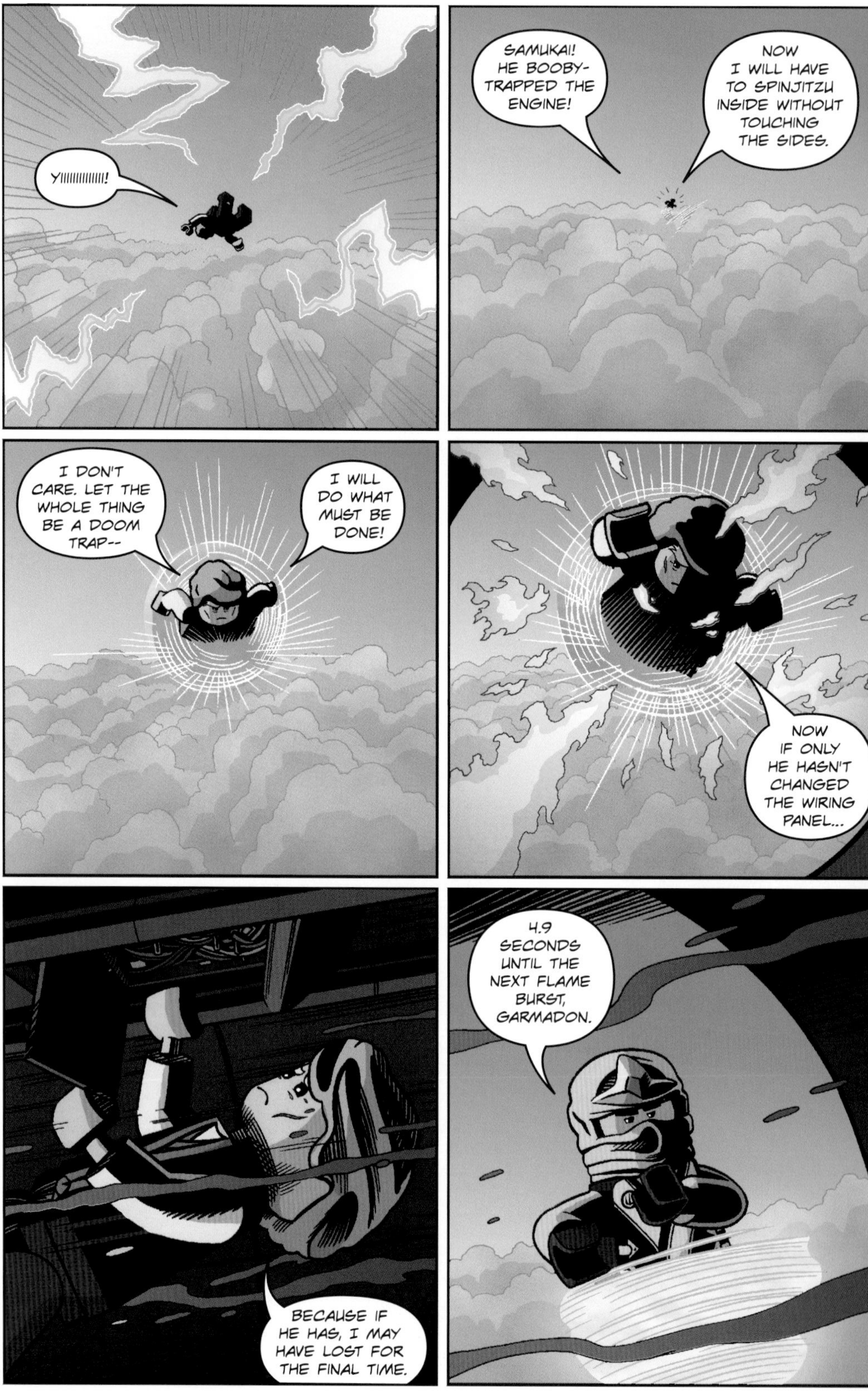
YIIIIIIIIIIII!
SAMUKAI! HE BOOBY-TRAPPED THE ENGINE!
NOW I WILL HAVE TO SPINJITZU INSIDE WITHOUT TOUCHING THE SIDES.
I DON'T CARE. LET THE WHOLE THING BE A DOOM TRAP--
I WILL DO WHAT MUST BE DONE!
NOW IF ONLY HE HASN'T CHANGED THE WIRING PANEL...
BECAUSE IF HE HAS, I MAY HAVE LOST FOR THE FINAL TIME.
4.9 SECONDS UNTIL THE NEXT FLAME BURST, GARMADON.

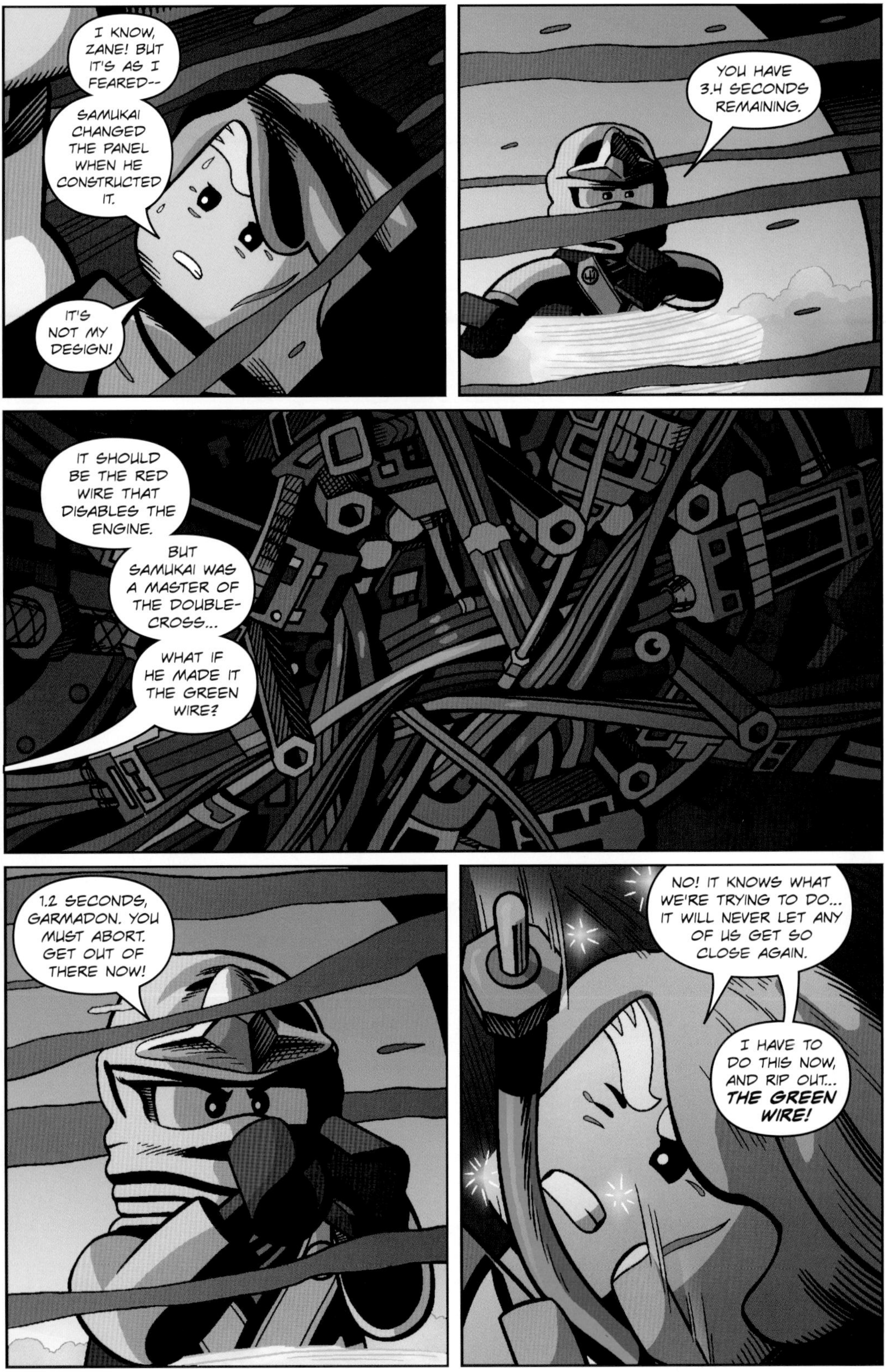
I KNOW, ZANE! BUT IT'S AS I FEARED--
SAMUKAI CHANGED THE PANEL WHEN HE CONSTRUCTED IT.
IT'S NOT MY DESIGN!
YOU HAVE 3.4 SECONDS REMAINING.
IT SHOULD BE THE RED WIRE THAT DISABLES THE ENGINE.
BUT SAMUKAI WAS A MASTER OF THE DOUBLE-CROSS...
WHAT IF HE MADE IT THE GREEN WIRE?
1.2 SECONDS, GARMADON. YOU MUST ABORT. GET OUT OF THERE NOW!
NO! IT KNOWS WHAT WE'RE TRYING TO DO... IT WILL NEVER LET ANY OF US GET SO CLOSE AGAIN.
I HAVE TO DO THIS NOW, AND RIP OUT... ***THE GREEN WIRE!***

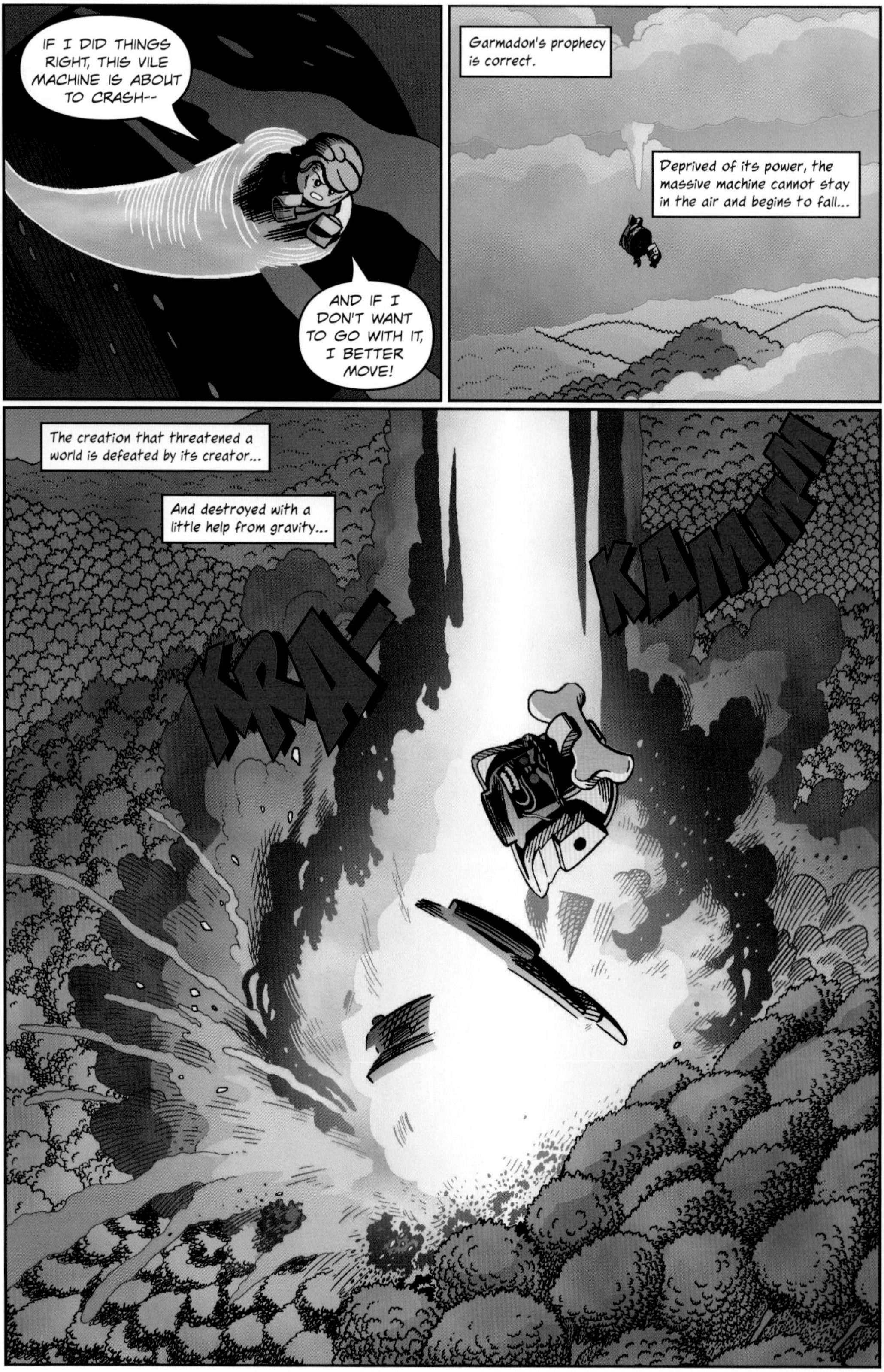
IF I DID THINGS RIGHT, THIS VILE MACHINE IS ABOUT TO CRASH--
AND IF I DON'T WANT TO GO WITH IT, I BETTER MOVE!
Garmadon's prophecy is correct.
Deprived of its power, the massive machine cannot stay in the air and begins to fall...
The creation that threatened a world is defeated by its creator...
And destroyed with a little help from gravity...
KRA-
KAMMMM

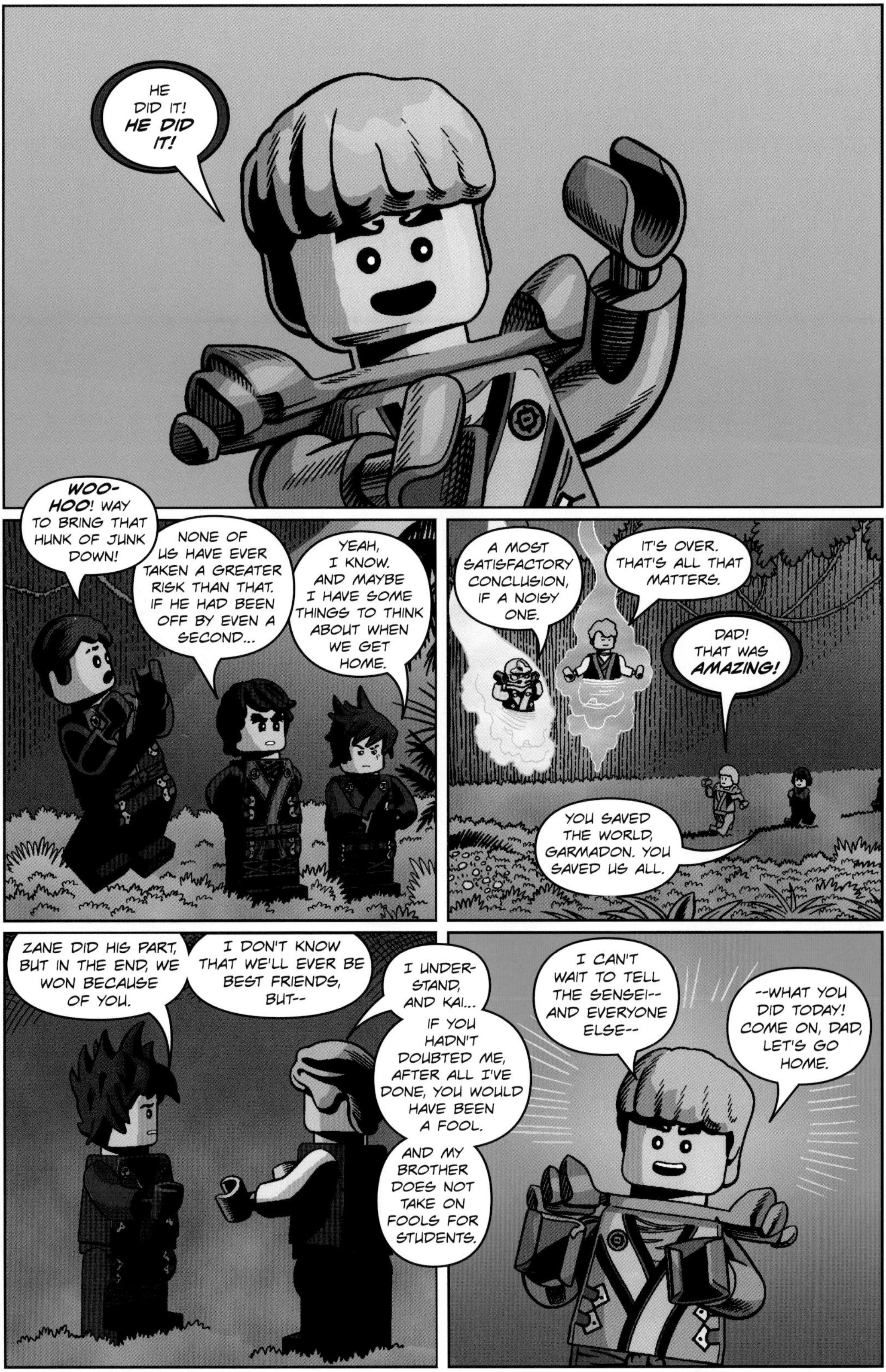
HE DID IT! HE DID IT!
WOO-HOO! WAY TO BRING THAT HUNK OF JUNK DOWN!
NONE OF US HAVE EVER TAKEN A GREATER RISK THAN THAT. IF HE HAD BEEN OFF BY EVEN A SECOND...
YEAH, I KNOW. AND MAYBE I HAVE SOME THINGS TO THINK ABOUT WHEN WE GET HOME.
A MOST SATISFACTORY CONCLUSION, IF A NOISY ONE.
IT'S OVER. THAT'S ALL THAT MATTERS.
DAD! THAT WAS AMAZING!
YOU SAVED THE WORLD, GARMADON. YOU SAVED US ALL.
ZANE DID HIS PART, BUT IN THE END, WE WON BECAUSE OF YOU.
I DON'T KNOW THAT WE'LL EVER BE BEST FRIENDS, BUT--
I UNDER-STAND, AND KAI...
IF YOU HADN'T DOUBTED ME, AFTER ALL I'VE DONE, YOU WOULD HAVE BEEN A FOOL.
AND MY BROTHER DOES NOT TAKE ON FOOLS FOR STUDENTS.
I CAN'T WAIT TO TELL THE SENSEI-- AND EVERYONE ELSE--
--WHAT YOU DID TODAY! COME ON, DAD, LET'S GO HOME.

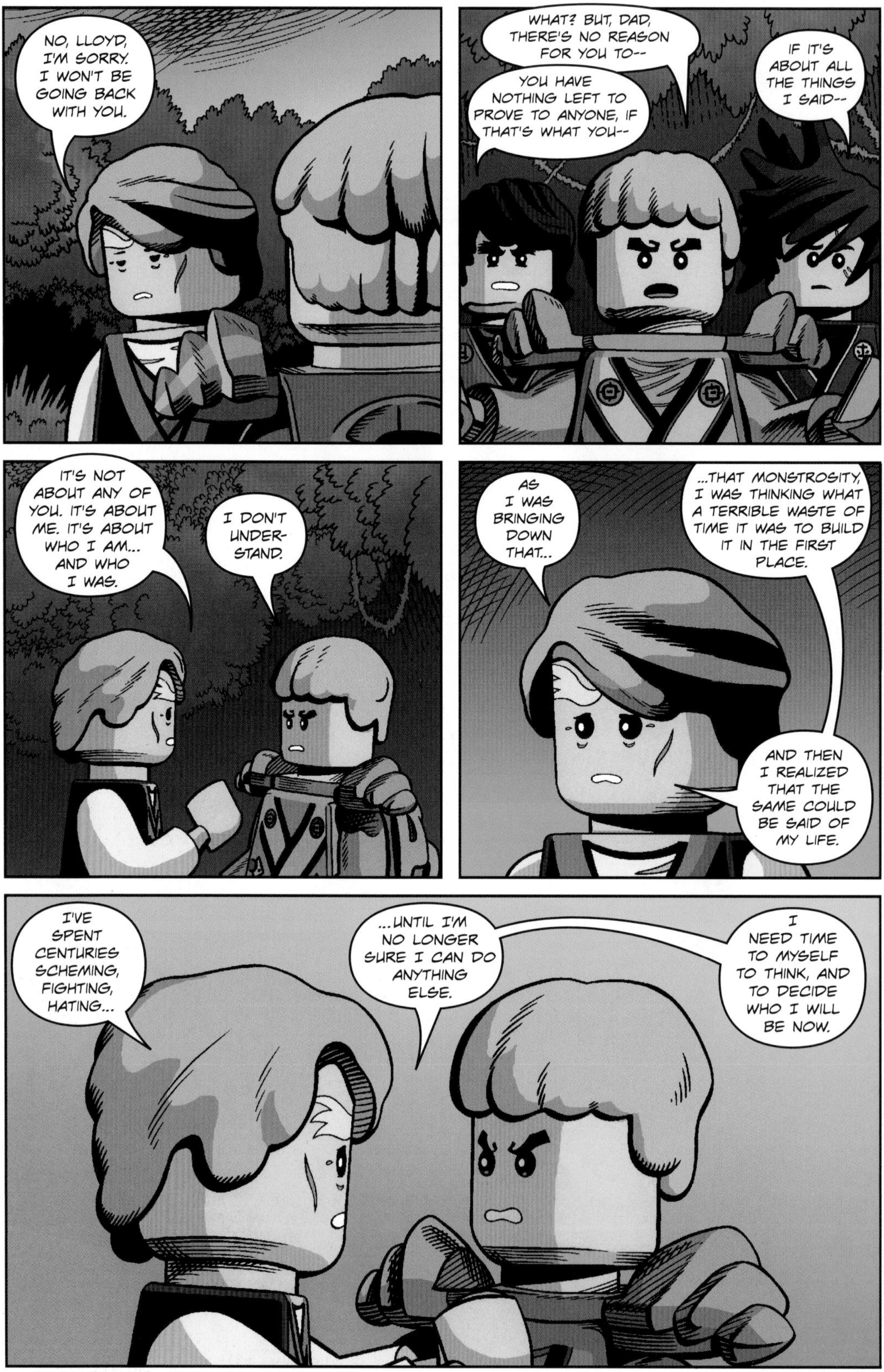
NO, LLOYD, I'M SORRY. I WON'T BE GOING BACK WITH YOU.
WHAT? BUT, DAD, THERE'S NO REASON FOR YOU TO--
YOU HAVE NOTHING LEFT TO PROVE TO ANYONE, IF THAT'S WHAT YOU--
IF IT'S ABOUT ALL THE THINGS I SAID--
IT'S NOT ABOUT ANY OF YOU. IT'S ABOUT ME. IT'S ABOUT WHO I AM... AND WHO I WAS.
I DON'T UNDER-STAND.
AS I WAS BRINGING DOWN THAT...
...THAT MONSTROSITY, I WAS THINKING WHAT A TERRIBLE WASTE OF TIME IT WAS TO BUILD IT IN THE FIRST PLACE.
AND THEN I REALIZED THAT THE SAME COULD BE SAID OF MY LIFE.
I'VE SPENT CENTURIES SCHEMING, FIGHTING, HATING...
...UNTIL I'M NO LONGER SURE I CAN DO ANYTHING ELSE.
I NEED TIME TO MYSELF TO THINK, AND TO DECIDE WHO I WILL BE NOW.

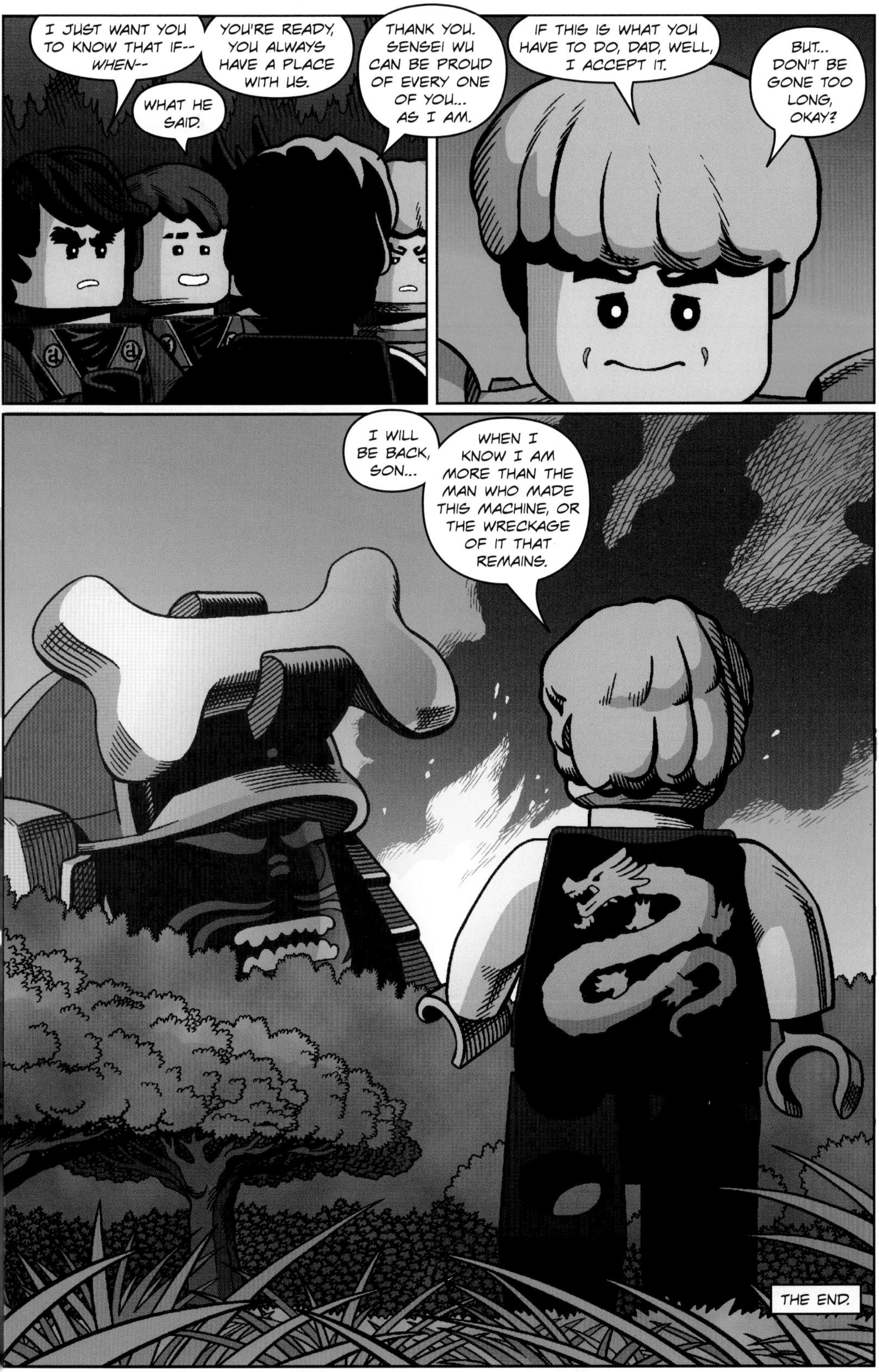
I JUST WANT YOU TO KNOW THAT IF-- WHEN--
WHAT HE SAID.
YOU'RE READY, YOU ALWAYS HAVE A PLACE WITH US.
THANK YOU. SENSEI WU CAN BE PROUD OF EVERY ONE OF YOU... AS I AM.
IF THIS IS WHAT YOU HAVE TO DO, DAD, WELL, I ACCEPT IT.
BUT... DON'T BE GONE TOO LONG, OKAY?
I WILL BE BACK, SON...
WHEN I KNOW I AM MORE THAN THE MAN WHO MADE THIS MACHINE, OR THE WRECKAGE OF IT THAT REMAINS.
THE END.

WATCH OUT FOR PAPERCUTZ™

Welcome to the enlightening, engaging, and inevitably entrapping eighth LEGO® NINJAGO graphic novel from Papercutz, the deconstructed comics company dedicated to publishing great graphic novels for all ages! I'm your Green (Ninja) Tea-sipping Editor-in-Chief, Jim Salicrup just back from the Biggest Comicbook Show on Earth! Of course I'm talking about the 2013 Comic-Con International.

Like last year, we were honored again when the Hageman Brothers, the brilliant writers of the animated LEGO Ninjago Cartoon Network TV series, stopped by the Papercutz booth to pick up the new LEGO Ninjago poster by Jolyon Yates. They both shared a few exciting secrets about the future of LEGO Ninjago, but since we're sworn to secrecy we can't tell you anything except the best is yet to come for our favorite masters of Spinjitzu!

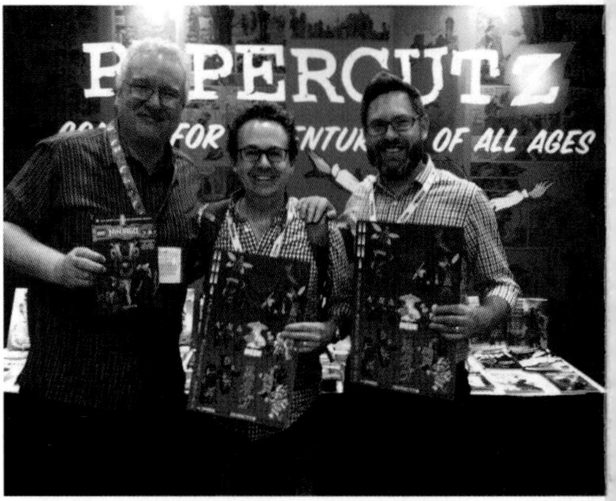

Jim with Kevin and Dan Hageman. Or is it Dan and Kevin?

Of course, Jolyon Yates was also at the Papercutz booth (along with our Marketing Director Jesse Post, Production Coordinator Beth Scorzato, and Publisher Terry Nantier) signing posters, and on Sunday, drawing lots of free sketches of Jay, Cole, Zane, and Kai. Seeing all the enthusiastic LEGO NINJAGO fans was great fun and it re-energized us all. We're working harder than ever to make the upcoming LEGO NINJAGO graphic novels better than anything you've seen so far! For example, we've got a bonus Lloyd story planned for LEGO NINJAGO #9! That should be available around the same time as The LEGO Movie is released—which in addition to appearances by Batman, Superman, Wonder Woman, a Teenage Mutant Ninja Turtle (Leonardo), and others, also features the Green Ninja!

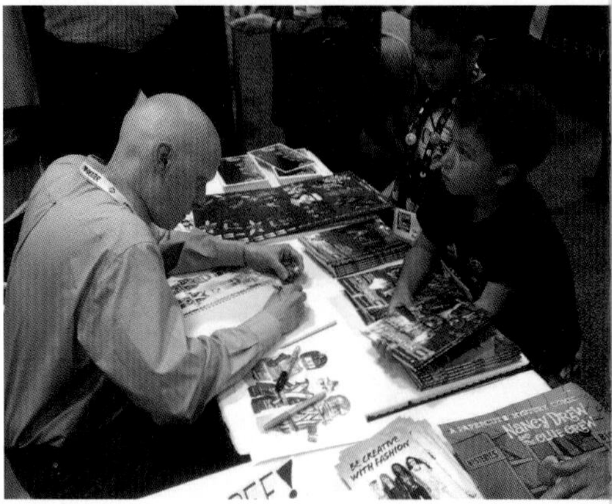

Jolyon Yates drawing crowds and ninja at the Papercutz booth.

So, until next time, keep spinnin'! Ninja-GO!

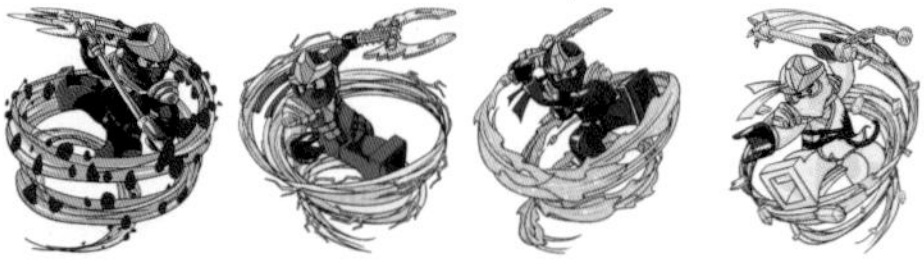

Jim

STAY IN TOUCH!

EMAIL:	salicrup@papercutz.com
WEB:	papercutz.com
TWITTER:	@papercutzgn
FACEBOOK:	PAPERCUTZGRAPHICNOVELS
SNAIL MAIL:	Papercutz, 160 Broadway, Suite 700, East Wing, New York, NY 10038